The Hand That Feeds You

Some Call it Death.

Others Call it Love.

Tim Baker

The Hand That Feeds You

NORMANDIE PRESS
Books. Unbound.

This story is a work of fiction. All contents, including: names, characters, places, incidents, and all references herein, are the work of the author. Any resemblance to actual persons, living or dead, events or locales is purely coincidental.

Copyright © 2022 Tim Baker

Cover Image: Jorge Fakhouri Filho

Cover Design: Tim Baker

Book Design: Tim Baker

All rights reserved. No part of this publication may be reproduced, distributed, or transmitted in any form or by any means, without the prior, written consent of the author and/or publisher, except for brief quotations which may be used for a book review and certain other non-commercial uses permitted under copyright law.

First Edition (Paperback, Hardback, and eBook for Kindle) December 2022

ISBN: 9798366090308 (Paperback)

ISBN: 9798366733748 (Hardback)

DEDICATION

This book is dedicated to my mother, who crossed from this world, into the next, twenty years ago; yet has never, truly left me. I'd also like to dedicate this to all of my supportive family, friends, and of course the countless cups of coffee that endured me throughout the journey of writing this book; without whom, this story would still be sitting around half-finished on a hard-drive, somewhere. Thank you.

Stay Skeptical.

PROLOGUE

Welcome, dear reader, I'm glad you're here. Not just here, as in reading this story, but *here*, as in starting your journey at the very beginning.

The Prologue has become somewhat of a lost art form. Forlorn. Forgotten. Forsaken by modern readers for the chance to dive right into the action, with *Chapter One*.

Don't misunderstand, my friend, as the keeper of this tale, I don't judge. I've been guilty of cracking open a virgin title and bypassing everything until I reach the first page of the first chapter; more times than I care to admit.

The overly-anxious peruser will still be able to understand and enjoy our story, but you, *dear reader*, will have a deeper understanding, richer context, and more pieces of the puzzle to put together as the tale unfolds.

THE HAND THAT FEEDS YOU

This portion of our story will be spent unpacking the enigma that is Hollingshead, Maine.

Situated on the Eastern Coast of the Atlantic, about an hour or so from Bangor, it possesses the same, quaint charm, generations of devoted tourists, and breath-taking scenery of many a New England town.

You've never heard of it, you say? You're not alone. Despite its throngs of annual visitors, Hollingshead is a town that keeps a low profile; and for very good reason.

Created at the hands of the affluent, *for* the affluent, governed and controlled *by* the affluent since its inception, in the mid-nineteenth century; little has changed in the last hundred and fifty years.

Once a prominent port city, its wealth came from an endless supply of commercial goods, both imported as well as those produced locally; which would be loaded onto railroad cars and shipped all across the young, American continent.

While the town was more than eager to share its wares with the world, it's never been one to share itself. That is to say, the town has never been open to outsiders. In fact, there's an old saying that locals used to joke about this very thing, that went: *if you want to move to Hollingshead, you need an invitation.*

This is where our story begins.

In 1850, a young couple by the name of Gheata left their native Romania and emigrated to America, in search of the "American dream."

The prosperous nation was booming, thanks to an industrial revolution, the likes of which the world had never seen. Many families, just like the Gheatas, left their old lives behind, certain that they might become the next Andrew Carnegie.

Mr. Gheata, who was filled with more dream than ambition, had been without steady employment for over a year. After his wife discovered that she was pregnant, he convinced her that a fresh start would be just the thing they needed. So, they boarded an ocean liner, bound for New York.

After a few years of living in unsanitary tenement housing, realizing that there was a good reason it was called the "American *dream*," Mr. Gheata, his wife, and their three year old son, whom they named Carlisle, left the crowded metropolis, heading for a small village in Maine. Here the couple had found stable employment; he working at the docks for a wealthy shipping merchant, and she as a servant, in the merchant's impressive estate.

THE HAND THAT FEEDS YOU

While their livelihood was now putting ample food on the table, the distance between the couple's lives was growing more and more widespread, with each year that ticked away.

With her husband spending the majority of his time at the docks, and the rest of his time at the bar, Mrs. Gheata would assume the role of father and mother, to young Carlisle; something which fueled the hatred she had grown to harbor for her husband. America wasn't the promised land that he'd sold her on, all those years ago. She couldn't afford to take her son and return back to her beloved Romania, even if the stigma of divorce weren't a social death-sentence, at that time.

So, if she couldn't bring her son to his home, she would bring that home to him. Throughout his childhood, Carlisle's mother would share stories about his native homeland, about its mystère and its magic. And, every night, she would sing him a lullaby that her mother had sang to her, and her mother before that; all in the hopes that her son wouldn't forget where he came from. Sure, he may've been born an American, learned to speak the language so that he sounded just like everyone else,

"But you'll always be a Romanian, deep *in here*," his mother would say.

Then she'd gently pat his chest, over his heart.

Despite his love for his mother, Carlisle was also heavily-influenced by his father. If Mrs. Gheata had wished for her son to return to his roots, Mr. Gheata wished for his son to plant those roots in America. Despite the harsh reality that almost no one actually becomes a millionaire, the hope that they *could* was enough to perpetuate the dream. It may've been *nearly impossible*, but at least it was *possible*.

Instead of sharing stories of dark and dreary Romania, Carlisle's father would tell him stories about the elite clubs in New York, the money that men made on Wall Street, and the lavish lifestyle that he had seen being around his employer, Mr. Cartwright.

Like his father, Carlisle had an insatiable urge to fit in with high society. He'd inherited that oh-so-charming, and dangerous, propensity for dreaming about having more money than he could ever spend in one lifetime, ensuring that the world knew his name, and even rubbing shoulders with the powerful men who controlled every aspect of modern society.

The strange dichotomy of his parents, two very different halves of the same whole, took root in Carlisle; often causing him to be at odds with his own self.

THE HAND THAT FEEDS YOU

Now in his mid-twenties, with his father dead of an overly-abused liver, and his mother of tuberculosis, Carlisle was now left completely alone. Deciding to walk in his father's footsteps, he made the move back to New York, adopting the surname of his father's old employer, *Cartwright*, in an effort to sound more more distinguished, more *American*. His father had always told him,

"It's all about appearances, Carlisle. It's all about playing the game. If you can convince them that you live in their world, they'll hand you the keys."

With his dashing good looks and his devilish charm, he was able to gain access to their club. After only a few short months in the city, he'd already secured himself a string of high-profile friends; friends who could foot the bill for their expensive luncheons, their vintage nightcaps, their exclusive dinner parties.

But, being a side-kick wasn't good enough. No, he not only wanted to be one of them, he wanted to be envied by them. But how could he do that? He lacked the financial resources. His mouth lacked that fabled silver spoon with which they'd all been born. He needed a plan. A money-making scheme.

Business start-ups required money, money that he

didn't have, *obviously*. What he needed was an invention. Something that no one else had dreamt up, yet. But what? It had to be cheap. It had to be something he could easily produce himself. It had to be something that would sell.

He began with elixirs. They were easy. Miracle cures that were merely sugar-water, with a bit of coloring to convince its patients that it was a legitimate cure-all. His charm made him a natural salesman. Through this he was able to get enough seed money to dream bigger.

Much bigger.

His next move was an invention that was going to revolutionize the world, it was an early form of the electric light bulb; a version which predated the incandescent prototype released by Edison and his team at Menlo Park.

This was during a global race to invent the first, commercially-viable, electric light. Inventors across the globe were pouring their lives into this; certain it would make them America's next tycoon.

When Carlisle invited his friends over for a dinner party, he promised them magic like they'd never seen before. Sure enough, he delivered. The guests were welcomed into a house lit entirely by candlelight, and after serving dinner, he ordered his housekeeper to blow out every candle; leaving he and his guests in total darkness. A few of them shrieked, afraid of the dark; bidding him to relight the candles, accusing Carlisle of taking a silly joke too far.

Then, *gasps*.

Every room of the house became illuminated by the mere flip of a switch; as if by magic. Just as promised.

His guests were practically climbing over each other to grab their checkbooks. Each hopeful to invest in this incredible opportunity. Each trying to out-invest the other.

And, just like that, Carlisle Cartwright became America's newest millionaire. Everything went according to plan. Everything worked perfectly.

Too perfectly.

Unfortunately, before he officially went public with his new venture, it was discovered that Carlisle had "borrowed," not only research data, but materials from an acquaintance who worked at a certain research facility in Menlo Park; employed by, none other than, *Thomas Edison, himself*.

If you didn't know, Edison had a huge ego. While this theory has been widely-debated, many historians suggest that he didn't *actually* invent things, but rather he opened his pocketbook so that others could; then, having funded the inventions, he took full credit for them. So, when word got out that Cartwright's electric light was made possible by Edison's work, let's just say that Carlisle's fortune went as quickly as it had come.

More than that, he was ruined. Not just financially, but socially as well. See, all of his friends who'd invested in his business had also lost *their* money on the venture.

Lots of money.

So, in 1875, with his reputation shot, without more than a couple bucks to his name, Carlisle used what little he had to purchase a one-way ticket to his native Romania. He didn't know what he'd do there, but he figured that he could try his hand at rebuilding his fortune with some fresh blood.

In less than a month, Carlisle had taken a job as a dock-worker for a wealthy merchant; *ironic*, right? But, unlike his father, he knew this wasn't permanent, it was just a foot in the door.

You see, the merchant had taken a great liking to Carlisle. He had always been fascinated with America, and Western culture, so he treated his young employee more like a son; constantly asking questions about and begging to hear stories of that strange and exciting world across the Atlantic.

That's not all. The merchant also had a daughter. A

beautiful daughter, named Belinda. By now, you, no doubt, know that Carlisle was nothing if not an opportunist. If he where able to marry Belinda, he would stand to inherit a fortune. It was almost too easy.

Belinda's father wasn't willing to let just anyone marry his daughter. Despite the fondness he had for Carlisle, the boy had no money. What could he offer to ensure that she'd be taken care of, financially? This was gonna be harder than he thought.

One day, while working on the docks, daydreaming instead of focusing on his work, *as usual*, he began thinking about the invention that had once been his ticket to the top. The thing that he'd lost before he actually had. What if there was still something he could do with it? Electricity could be useful for more than just light, *couldn't it*?

He looked up at the black smoke coming out of the funnels on the small, merchant vessel. It was dirty. Casting a mess of black grime upon everything and everyone in its path. And the smell, he hated the smell.

Too bad there's not a better way to generate steam.

Well, there is oil, but it's expensive.

Wait a minute. Of course!

That's when it came to him. Electricity could be used

for heating. It was cheap to produce in bulk, heated instantly, and could warm an entire apartment building if the plumbing were routed properly. His mind jumped from one possibility to the next. It could do so many things.

When Carlisle's employer received a request for a business meeting, from one of his employees, he was a bit skeptical. If it were anyone else, he'd have said *no*, but he liked this kid, so he'd at least give him an opportunity to present whatever idea he had; no matter how banal it surely was.

Back in his element, Carlisle controlled the room, impressing his boss and a few investors he'd brought along to hear the boy's pitch. The kid was a natural. He'd made notes to pass around, gathered statistics, had a business model and a game plan. The men were impressed. More than that, they were sold. Carlisle had, once again, been given carte blanche to proceed with his latest invention. Only, this time, everything went according to plan.

Carlisle was once again a millionaire.

Because of this, he now had permission to marry Belinda, further solidifying his financial footing; as he now had access to, not only *his* funds, but the funds of a limitless financial network. He was back in *the club*.

With his new-found fortune, and his beautiful wife, life seemed good for Carlisle. But, what he really longed for was a family. A child, or a house-full of children, that he could spoil. To give them the life, the childhood that he'd always wished for himself.

Sadly, after suffering a string of miscarriages, Belinda's doctor told her that she might never have children; going so far as to warn her that her next attempt at pregnancy might just result in sepsis, which would likely kill her.

Fearing that her handsome and charismatic husband might soon lose interest if she couldn't give him the children he so desperately wanted, Belinda devised a plan. She could pay someone to have a child for her. But, it would have to be someone who would keep the matter quiet; someone who could be controlled.

Camilla was one of Belinda's chambermaids. With her dark hair and strong features, she was a striking beauty. Someone that, Belinda assumed, would produce beautiful offspring.

When Belinda first told her husband of her idea, he dismissed it.

"It's just, too messy," he told her.

That was *until* he saw Camilla. He loved his wife. He

adored her beauty. But, she was someone safe. Angelic. Something about Camilla struck Carlisle in a way that he'd never felt before. Suddenly, the desire to be able to have sex with another woman, a mysterious woman like Camilla, was all the persuasion he needed.

Of course he didn't tell his wife this. But women are inherently discerning. Belinda noticed signs. Lots of them. After the deed was done, Camilla started venturing into different areas of the house. Areas that she normally would've *never* been in. Areas where she had no business. Areas where *Carlisle* was present.

One day, Belinda walked into the study and found Camilla and Carlisle talking. The maid was wearing makeup. Perhaps she always had, but Belinda had never noticed it until that moment. Her face became hot with anger, but she held her tongue well. Instead of spouting-off, she made up some story about Camilla being needed in the kitchen.

With the woman safely out of ear's shot, Belinda scolded her husband.

"I don't like it," she said, coldly.

"What?"

"The way you look at her."

"What are you talking—"

"I'm not blind, Carlisle!"

"You're letting your imagination run wild."

"Am I? Apparently I'm not the only one. I've overheard the other servants talking."

Her husband didn't respond. He just let his gaze drop to the floor, but said nothing.

"It ends, *now*. Do you hear me, Carlisle?"

Silence.

"Or, so help me, I will tell my father and he'll see to it that you lose every—"

"*Fine!*"

He grabbed his wife, forcefully by the arms. This was the first time he'd ever been physically aggressive towards her. She was frightened. But she didn't let it show.

"Thank you, Carlisle. We'll never speak of this again."

Without another word from either, she left the room, leaving her husband alone with his thoughts. She stole safely to a dark corner of the hallway and silently wept. Wondering what he may've done had she pushed him harder.

Turns out, she had good reason to worry about the relationship between her maid and her husband. Carlisle was not only infatuated with Camilla, he was falling in love with her. Some part of her felt right. She felt like home. Maybe it's because he *was home*. Being here, in *Romania*, the land where his mother drew inspiration for her dark, bedtime stories. With a woman that carried the same love and voracity for the dark and the strange, as his mother had. Things that were considered taboo for someone with an American upbringing. Or at least they were supposed to feel that way. They didn't feel that way to him.

Carlisle may've had his father's love of money, but he had his mother's openness to the things that were mysterious. Something which he and Camilla had discussed, at length, the night they'd spent together. Something which both he and she longed to experience again. Something which, in secret, they *had* done again. And again.

After it was determined that Camilla was *indeed* pregnant, Belinda had decided that, once the child was born, the woman was to be fired; cut out of their lives forever.

Camilla, on the other hand, had very different plans. She wasn't about to leave the Cartwright home. In fact, she'd promised herself that, in one way or another, she would take Belinda's place. She *would be* Mrs. Carlisle Cartwright.

In the months that followed, blood ran ice cold, and tempers raged white hot around the manor. Everyone was on pins and needles. Everyone knew the truth. Carlisle was sleeping with his mistress. Some said that she'd cast a spell upon him; for it was well-known that she knew a little magic. Carlisle's ego delighted in the fact that he had two women fighting over him; each convinced that they'd the be one he ultimately chose.

About a month or so before the child was to be born, a small uprising had begun making waves in Romania. A group of protesters (sympathizers of *The Wallachian Revolution of 1848*) had started a grassroots movement; hellbent on abolishing all of the country's ties to the once-present rule of Russia. Anyone with ties to the Czar or his family, which was most all of the old-money aristocracy, was targeted.

Eventually the movement scaled from the destruction of property, to the taking of lives. At first the Cartwrights remained put; resolute that the whole ordeal would blow over in time. But after one of the servants was attacked and killed by rioters, Carlisle made the decision that it was time to take his family and escape to America.

The Cartwrights settled in Hollingshead in the summer of 1880; opting to build their mansion high on the coast, overlooking the sea. Life had come full-circle for Carlisle; full-circle *indeed*. He was determined to flaunt his wealth in the faces of the very people who'd once belittled he and his family for being members of the working-class.

From the magnificent castle that loomed high on the mountain, which he called *Hawthorne Manor*, to the lavish parties that he hosted there, Carlisle's name was now synonymous with wealth in excess. New money or not, try as they might, the upper echelon of Hollingshead could not ignore the Cartwright name.

Despite this, they were not accepting. Belinda was foreign. She spoke perfect English, but there was something slightly off about it. She wasn't one of them. Nor was her mysterious maidservant that she'd brought with her, from across the sea.

That's right, much to the chagrin of her mistress, Camilla was still very much pregnant when the Cartwrights made their escape. So, they had no choice but to take her with them; something Belinda regretted allowing. She should've just let the child go. She could find a way to secure another. Hire someone else for a similar arrangement, but Carlisle was adamant, Camilla would be coming with them. End of discussion.

After the child was born, both women would find it difficult to cope with being the mother of a child that wasn't truly theirs. A child that existed to bridge the gap between themselves and the man that they loved. A child that they'd unknowingly brainwash, manipulating the girl, *Isabella*, to love them; all in hopes that winning her love and affection, would secure the love of Carlisle as well.

If Bella chose them, then maybe, *just maybe*, Carlisle would choose them.

Or so the legend says.

Alright, we've discussed the history of Hollingshead; now it's time for us to move on to the character that's woven into the very core of our diegesis.

To begin, you *must know* that this book tells the story of a woman named Andie Sterling.

Andie is many things. She's a bestselling author. Her tales of horror have delighted and terrified countless readers over the course of her decade-long career. With a delicate balance of semi-formal prose and genuine, conversational style, her voice has been praised by her critics and her peers, alike; many comparing her voice to that of her literary idol, Stephen King.

What else can I tell you about Andie?

She's quick-witted and adventurous. Never shying away from a good dare, or chasing down a solid story. She's also sarcastic, sometimes downright savage; and yet, she's got a sweet, tender side. This is something she only shows with those in whom she wholeheartedly trusts.

So, we've talked about what Andie *is*, now let's discuss what Andie *isn't*.

Andie Sterling is *not* from Hollingshead, Maine. She has no family in Hollingshead. In fact, she'd never even heard of the town until about a month ago. So, why have we bothered to discuss it?

To understand Andie, you must first understand Hollingshead. You see, even though the two of them live in their own, separate worlds, they're eternally-linked, they just don't know it, *yet*. However, once their paths cross, both the woman, and the town, their past, present, and futures will be *forever* changed.

So, my friend, please remember what I've told you about Andie. I know it isn't much, but it'll serve you well as you continue discovering her journey within these pages.

THE HAND THAT FEEDS YOU

CHAPTER 1

His back was to her. That didn't matter. The bar was also dark; very dark. Again, it didn't matter. Did it matter that he was all the way across the room from the doorway where she stood? Nope, not even a little. None of it mattered, because she knew it was him. No question. She probably knew him better than she'd ever known anyone else in her life. If all of that weren't enough, she'd seen him nearly every day for the last four years. But not like this. *Never* like this.

He was always the one talking. Always the first one to say something sarcastic. It was his humor. It was his love language. When he threw some, playful, yet scathing zinger at you, you knew that you really meant something to him. You mattered. The alternative was all business. Cold. Stifled.

Forgettable. Andie shivered at the thought. He'd been all business with her ever since he got the call that his dad was in the hospital. It was sudden. It was unexpected. Neither he nor his mother could've imagined that his dad, a healthy, active man of only sixty two could go from hiking Pikes Peak to laying in a hospital bed, tethered to life support, in only a matter of a week. Even the doctors were left scratching their heads; disagreeing on his diagnosis. Taking bets on the outcome. *Whoever chose sudden death is a few bucks richer tonight.* None of it made any sense.

But, none of that mattered now. The only thing that mattered was to make sure he was OK. Andie didn't know what to say in situations like this. Sentiment was something that was genuinely lost on her. She'd never been close to her family, so all of the emotions that one should feel when losing a family member, it was foreign territory. She could write about emotions, sure, as long as it was fiction. But this, this was real life. This was a friend; someone that she cared about, deeply. Perhaps the only person she *truly* cared for.

When she passed by the casket then stopped to give him a quick, somber hug, he pulled her in tight. She'd never felt that type of connection with anyone before; at least not that she could remember. She didn't know if she liked it or not, but in that moment, she silently vowed to give him whatever he needed to be OK. She drew in a deep sigh, this was the time to make good on that vow.

"How ya doin'?"

It was a stupid question. She cursed the very words as they left her lips. Clearly, she already knew the answer. Still, it was all she could think to convey, to this pitiful shell of a man that sat before her. His shoulders were still lurched forward, the way they had been through the entire funeral. He just sat there for a moment, as if gaining the strength to answer her, then slowly the barstool rotated to face her, bringing him along with it. His gaze was still planted on the floor, he couldn't muster the strength to look her in the eye.

"I still can't believe it. You know? I mean…I just…he was…he just…" his voice trailed off into the dark abyss of the bar.

"I know. I'm so sorry," she politely interjected in an effort to keep from hearing him start crying, again.

That was a sound she never wanted to hear again. *Ever*. He wasn't a crier. He was strong. Strong like she was; or at least he always had been. That's part of what drew Andie to him. From the moment they first met, it was like they spoke the same language.

"Yeah," was all he could reply.

His eyes were welling up; here came the tears. *Dammit, don't you dare!*

She took the empty stool next to him. Instinctively, she gently placed a hand on his back, just between his shoulder blades. He was warm. She could feel her own pulse through the palm of her hand. After a second, she began gently rubbing his back.

"Hey?"

No response.

"Look at me," she pleaded.

He looked up at her, she was certain it was the first time he'd looked at her all day.

"I've got you, OK? Anything you need…I'm here for you."

Although his eyes were red, and enveloped in tears; they carried within them a look of reassurance. As if, in that very moment, her few words of comfort were just exactly the thing he needed to hear.

Before either of them knew what was happening… before either of them could protest, they'd traded the dark, crowded bar, for the dark emptiness of his bedroom. A swanky, penthouse apartment in some Tribeca high-rise.

"Is this, OK?" he whispered gently.

His profile cast in silhouette, before the backdrop of glowing embers in the Carrara marble fireplace.

"Shhh," she replied, putting her fingertip to his lips.

Partially because this moment was all about him, giving him the attention, the distraction he needed to get through the night. Partially because if she took the time to think about it, she knew she'd object.

His hands were warm, and soft against her bare skin. She grazed her open palms, her bare feet against the silky smooth sheets. Probably Egyptian cotton. Probably a thousand thread count, *or higher*. He'd always had expensive taste. She was reminded of this when she breathed him in. The scent of his cologne was velvety sweet, and masculine all the same. Amber, Oud wood, and maybe vintage tobacco? She'd smelled him a million times before in the office, but always in passing. She'd never taken the time to really take him all in. But in this moment, she relished in it.

His body wrapped around her like a warm blanket. Supple lips gently caught the nape of her neck, and glided across her collarbone. Goosebumps drew up and down her arms, and from the back of her neck down her spine. He'd found the right spot. She was putty in his delicate hands. In his mouth. Whatever fragility she'd seen of him in the bar, was gone, at least in these feverish moments. He was aggressive. He was commandeering. He was incredible.

She was held in the powerful strength of his arms, the vice-like grasp of his sturdy hands. She felt her body rise and fall in the cadence of his body's rhythm. She'd had sex, plenty of times. But not like this. It was never like this. Is this how it was supposed to be? I mean, she kind of hoped so; she loved it. That's what terrified her.

When it was over, when they'd both taken tissues to clean themselves up, they instinctively, and silently, fell into position on their respective sides of the bed. No talking. No longing glances. No nothing. Just…silence.

Andie's heart was still beating from the rush of it all. She hoped he couldn't hear it. She worked to maintain the pace of her breathing. *This is it*, she told herself. A one-night-stand. A one time thing. No feelings. No friends with benefits. *Nothing*. She couldn't risk it. He was too important to her. She would wait for him to fall asleep, then quietly slip out before sunrise. Yeah, that's what she'd do. Better that way.

*****

"Andie…" a faint whisper in her ear woke her up.

THE HAND THAT FEEDS YOU

She hadn't even realized she'd fallen asleep. *Dammit, he must be after round two...* she thought. She hesitantly looked over at him out of her peripheral, but no, he was fast asleep. *Hmmm. Maybe it was a dream.* Well, since he was sleeping, she decided now was the right time to make her escape. Quietly, she went to sit up, that's when she realized that she couldn't move. *What the...?* Her arms, legs, every part of her body seemed to be strapped down to the bed. The only thing mobile was her eyes, which peered around the dark room for some kind of answer. That's when she saw it.

It was little more than a transparent, black mist that wafted about the room. The sound was like the buzzing of a fly, but so loud that it shook the walls, violently. Her eyes looked over at him.

"Max, wake up! Wake UP, *dammit!*"

She yelled at the top of her lungs...except she wasn't yelling. She wasn't saying *anything*. She couldn't make a sound. Or maybe she just couldn't hear herself over the buzzing of this...this...

Wait a minute! She remembered, she'd seen this before. It had been years, but she recognized it. This was the thing she'd been haunted by as a child. She'd locked it away in the dark recesses of her past, where it had remained safely tucked-away; out of sight, out of mind. But, somehow, here it was…unbridled, free, terrible. It was back for its revenge.

"Andie…Andie…" it was luring her.

"What do you want from me?!" she tried to say, but she still couldn't speak.

Just then the shadow dove under the foot of the bed. Andie watched in fear, certain it wasn't over. Slowly, the duvet began rising from the foot of the bed. The thing sailed beneath the covers like a shark's fin cutting through the waves, until it reached Andie, when the covers burst back- sending them flying across the room. Again she tried to say,

"What do you want from me?!"

This time, it responded to her, in a menacing whisper.

"You know why I'm here. You know what you have to do…"

It let out a deep, demonic cackle. Her heart was racing.

What does this thing want me to do?

Then, she felt herself begin to move. Even though she couldn't move, not by herself, she felt her body moving, as if she were a marionette, tethered together with strings, and those strings were being pulled by some invisible force. She rolled over, opened the drawer of the nightstand, and looked instinctively for something...*anything*...sharp. Something that, in the right hands, could be deadly. She didn't know why she was doing this. She didn't want to do this...but she couldn't help it. She felt the desire to do...whatever it was she was about to do. Her hands fell upon something. *This will work*, she thought. Her hands emerged from the drawer holding a large pair of scissors, their metal finish gleaming in the moonlight.

She licked her lips as she spread the shears and admired their sharp edges. *What the fuck?* What was happening to her? This, this wasn't her...*was it?* Then she realized she could move after all. She *was* moving. Had she been the one doing this all along? *No*...no, it couldn't have been. It was...it was...this thing. It was driving her to do this. She didn't want to...but...she *had* to. She looked over at him, still sound asleep, as if under some spell. She watched the gentle pulsing of his chest as he breathed. In and out. In and out...

"Come on, Andie...do it. *Do it!*"

The whisper had returned, it wasn't all just in her mind *after all*.

Something was driving her to do this. But, whatever it was, she couldn't refuse, she couldn't resist. She leaned over, and gently placed the edge of the scissors to his neck.

"Now…" the voice came again.

Her hands were trembling. Her heartbeat was so loud that her eardrums felt like they were about to burst. She didn't want to do this…but some part of her, somewhere deep and dark within her, wanted this. Craved this.

"Do it, *NOW!*" yelled the voice.

CHAPTER 2

"No!" she yelled, sitting up in the bed. But it wasn't his bed...this was *her* bed. Well, technically she was in her *Airbnb*...but she was safe. *He* was safe. It had all just been a dream.

But, it wasn't the first time she'd had it. Ever since she'd gotten here, she'd had that same dream. And each time, it was terrible. That's why she'd promised herself that she wouldn't go to sleep, not if she could help it. In fact she hadn't even realized she'd fallen asleep. All she could remember was writing in her journal, which lay next to her on the bedside table.

It's almost 3:30.

She knew Mrs. Tyler, the owner of the *Airbnb* would

have breakfast on the table by 4:00, since her husband left for work before sunrise. Groggily, she stumbled out of bed and into the bathroom.

Geez, I've got to get some sleep, she thought to herself, after an unwelcome glance in the mirror. The dark circles under her eyes told the secrets of her sleepless nights. She'd need to remember to put on some cream highlight to cover those bags. Pushing her hair back, she noticed her blonde roots coming through. *Shit.*

She opened her tote bag, and began setting out the tools to restore her auburn locks. For as long as she could remember, she'd cursed the fates for making her a blonde. They say blondes have more fun, but that certainly wasn't the case for Andie. Come to think of it, Jean Harlow, Marilyn Monroe, Britney Spears…she couldn't think of a single blonde who'd had an easy life. She'd always had to work hard to get anyone to take her seriously. She was a naturally beautiful woman, but for some reason this seemed to only cause her more grief. Apparently everyone thought you could only have beauty or brains; never both. The moment she began dyeing her hair, people began treating her differently. They respected her.

First she tried black, but that was just too extreme for

her fair skin. Next she tried brunette, but it still didn't look quite right against her complexion. Ultimately she found that *0032 Rich Auburn*, the one in the silver box, was just the right shade. It was natural-looking and didn't fade as quickly as the darker colors.

With the paraphernalia spread around the bathroom sink-like she was prepared to take part in some dark, satanic ritual, with her fingers safely tucked inside the cheap, plastic gloves, she spread the strands of her hair and began applying the dye from root to tip; massaging the color into her scalp. As she did this, she began planning out her day.

Today she would prod Mrs. Taylor for information about the town. She knew that Mrs. Taylor, Julia, hadn't been too forthcoming with the info when they chatted that first day, but Andie had been in town for five days now, and had gotten nowhere. Literally, not one freaking piece of evidence. No one could even corroborate the information she already had. It seemed as though either no one knew anything about the dark past of the town, or no one wanted to talk about it.

Was it all a mistake? Coming here? She hoped not. I mean, she'd undertaken a story with less of a lead than this. Hell, most of her stories had little to no truth behind them, they were just stories she'd made up in her childhood. This,

this was something *real*. Something tangible. A real-life mystery. Something that no one else had written about. Something that no one else really seemed to know about, at least outside of this town.

If it hadn't been for that cryptic email, she would never have even heard of Hollingshead. For a moment, she felt embarrassed that she'd even acted upon it. I mean, a poorly-written email, from an unknown sender, that simply said, "*13 lie dead, buried beneath a million secrets. the truth lies in Hollingshead.*" Attached was a black and white photo, hard to make out, but appeared to show the charred remains of a large, burned down house.

That was it. No names. No dates. No addresses... nothing to go on. But, it felt like enough, *somehow*. The house, though unintelligible in the overexposed photograph, seemed vaguely familiar. Perhaps Andie had seen a story about it before. She couldn't say why, but she knew there was a story there. She had to be the one to tell it. To expose some grave wrongdoing, and hold accountable those responsible. Today would be the day. She would get the answers she was looking for. Or, at the very least, she'd get her start.

"My goodness, you're up early," Mrs. Taylor was pouring her husband a cup of coffee, then returned the carafe back to the warmer.

"Yeah, I uh, couldn't sleep," Andie replied.

"The storm keep you up?" Mr. Taylor, Bennett, took the seat next to Andie, and began adding sugar to his black coffee.

"Storm?" Andie asked; confused as she'd heard nothing last night.

"You're kidding right? I thought the roof was gonna blow off this house," he laughed, moving on to the creamer. "This time of year, they happen almost every night."

"Oh, I had my earbuds in all night, guess that's why I didn't hear it."

"Those silly earbuds. They're gonna be the reason the next generation is deaf before they're 50, mark my words," Julia shot a disapproving glance at Andie.

"She always says the same thing to me," said Jordan, sheepishly.

Andie looked at Julia and her husband, then at Jordan. She remembered her parents talking about their disapproval of interracial relationships, how they weren't exactly against the relationship itself, but rather how it wasn't fair to their offspring. *"Bi-racial children are just not treated the same,"* her mother would say. In that moment, Andie couldn't say whether her mother was right or wrong about that, but in her eyes, those kids had likely won the genetic lottery; at least that could be said for Jordan.

He was probably 17 or 18, and was shy enough to suggest that he didn't realize just how handsome he was. With his perfectly tan skin and the lightest green eyes she'd ever seen, Andie knew all it would take is a little confidence, and there'd be no stopping this kid. But, she sensed he'd probably lived a pretty sheltered life. Julia was, by all accounts, a *Stepford Wife*. Everything in her house was perfectly in its place, and everything was routine and predictable. She didn't like things that were out of the ordinary or uncomfortable.

Bennett, on the other hand seemed sweet, and playful. A man-sized version of a twelve-year old kid. The kind who'd play a harmless prank on someone then laugh uncontrollably when he'd been found out.

"So, Mrs. Taylor..." Andie began.

"Julia, please."

"Sorry, Julia, you say you've lived in Hollingshead your entire life?"

"Sure have. My family has been here for generations. Our bloodline can be traced back all the way to this town's founding family, the Hollingshead clan. Settlers from Durham."

"Then you must know this town's history."

"Of course. My ancestors immigrated to the New World in the mid-sixteenth century—"

"Oh," Andie interrupted. "That's all very fascinating, but it's not quite the part of the town's history I was hoping to hear about."

Julia frowned, then recovered her smile.

"Oh? What was it you were *hoping to hear about?*"

Andie hesitated for a moment. She could tell Julia was on to her, and she could tell the conversation wasn't welcomed. Still, she was desperate. If anyone would know, surely Julia knew.

"I was hoping you could tell me about the disappearances. About the—"

"For goodness sake, why would a pretty little thing like you wanna hear any of those dreadful stories?"

"Just curious. I've been asking folks around town, but I—"

"You *what?!*" Julia snapped.

She seemed pissed. Andie hadn't seen her show this much emotion up until this moment. Whatever her reasons, she was serious about keeping this town's secrets. She regained her composure once more, then began.

"Sweetheart, listen, you're a guest. *Understand?* Not just in this house, but in *this town*. This town, like any old town, has its share of old ghost stories. But, they're just stories. Old wives' tales. None of them true."

"Then why—"

"But! Even if they *aren't* true, they've caused many of the families in this town a great deal of grief. Some of them have suffered for generations as a result of false allegations that arose simply because of idle gossip. The good folks of this town have worked hard to put those things in the past, and move on. Then, every once in a while someone comes along, trying to stir up the past. Trying to stick their nose where it *doesn't belong*. And, well, let's just say, it doesn't end up well for anyone. Do you understand what I'm telling you?"

Her tone was even and sweet, but her eyes assured Andie that this conversation was over.

"I, uh, understand," Andie relented.

"Atta girl," Julia smiled.

Then, Mrs. Taylor changed the conversation and went back to preparing piles of pancakes for the breakfast feast she sat before them.

Andie looked coyly across the table at Bennett and Jordan. Oddly enough, they looked as though they'd been the ones scolded, instead of Andie. She assumed they'd been on the wrong end of that conversation at least a time or two.

After breakfast, Andie thanked the Taylors for a delicious meal, then excused herself from the table. It was still an hour or so before sunrise, but she'd vowed not to waste another day; that and the fact that she now felt awkward sitting around making small-talk with her host family, namely *Julia*.

Andie was reaching for her car door when she heard someone whisper from behind.

"Hey..."

She turned around to find Jordan had followed her outside.

"Um, what are you doing out here? Shouldn't you be in—"

"They aren't just ghost stories. They're true. All of them," he said; with more authority than Andie'd ever heard Jordan speak.

"I don't think your mom would want you—"

"I don't care what she wants. She's a liar, just like

everyone in this town. They wanna bury the past to make themselves look good. But none of them are innocent. This whole town's got blood on its hands."

"What do you mean, Jordan? If you know something, please, tell me. I really wanna know."

Jordan looked over his shoulder, as if the devil himself were watching.

"I, I can't…" he began, "but, the mayor's wife, Eleanor Bond, she knows everything. Really into the dark stuff. Knows all the town's history. She's the one you'll wanna talk to."

He looked over his shoulder again.

"I've gotta go. Good luck, Ms. Sterling."

"*Andie*, please," she smiled.

Jordan blushed.

"*Andie*. I hope you find whatever it is that you're looking for."

He quietly turned and ventured back into the house.

"Me too, Jordan. Me *too*."

CHAPTER 3

Far across town from the modest, single family homes where the Taylor family lived and operated their *Airbnb*, just one block East of the courthouse square, there lies a small, sequestered area of town. Forest Grove, or as the locals call it Country Club Estates.

An historic community of old-money mansions, which sit atop their perfectly manicured lawns, each consisting of at least an acre. Prime real estate *indeed*. The streets only run North and South, with no cross-streets to interrupt them; each bearing the moniker of a flowering tree. Dogwood, Cherry, and Magnolia.

If you needed just one example of the exuberant wealth of this neighborhood; you could find it at 300 Magnolia Street. A stately three story, red brick, Georgian

Colonial. Her walls stand tall and proud; head and shoulders above all the rest. Clad in ivy, adorned with over-sized, flickering parsons lanterns, and neatly trimmed with tastefully-tarnished copper guttering and downspouts.

Not only a showstopper in her appointments, but also in scale. Something that didn't just happen by chance. Intentionally designed to be the largest house on the block. In the mid-nineteenth century Hollingshead was on the shortlist to become the state capital. The city's impressive courthouse originally intended to serve as the capitol building, and 300 Magnolia, the governor's mansion.

But it was never meant to be. Hollingshead's dreams of grandeur soon faded as it lost its hopeful title to Augusta. The capitol was demoted to a mere courthouse. And although the splendid mansion never called itself the residence of the most powerful elected official in the state, it would find solace in accommodating the most powerful elected official in the city; the mayor.

On this particular morning, around the time Andie was heading down to join her hosts for breakfast, Mrs. Bond was preparing breakfast in the large, well-appointed kitchen of 300 Magnolia.

Eleanor Bond had descended from the bloodline of the

Vanderbilts; one of the wealthiest families in American history. When her great-great grandfather brought the railroad into the far Northeastern Territory, before Maine was incorporated as a state, he settled with his family in the area that would later become Hollingshead. He'd chosen this undeveloped land with the intention of going into politics and carving out the state governorship for himself. While those plans never came to fruition, the family remained, and their wealth and influence became an integral part of the town's history.

Named after one of the pioneers of the American feminist movement, Eleanor Roosevelt, her mother had hoped that, like her namesake, Eleanor would be strong, independent, and outspoken in the face of adversity; a shining beacon (or at least a squeaky wheel) in an overwhelmingly patriarchal society; and she certainly was. Her husband, the mayor, knew this.

Historically Eleanor's family, most notably her grandmother, had been very involved in the *Spiritualist Movement*. That love of mysticism and the occult had been instilled into Eleanor since childhood, and it was something which she was still vehemently passionate about. Not only did she feel strongly-connected with the spirit world, but often claimed herself to be clairvoyant. Because of these beliefs she often found herself at odds with the pious, Protestant upper echelon of the town. As mayor, her husband was certainly vocal about his protest towards her beliefs; or at the very least discussing them publicly.

While personally, he couldn't care one way or another what form of religion his wife practiced, I mean hell, he was probably more of an atheist than anything, but modern society looked down upon the strange beliefs of spiritualism. For them, religion had evolved into something much more tame. Something safe. They'd filtered out the bad and kept what they'd deemed good.

For them, God was a loving, white-haired, benevolent grandfather, more like Santa Claus, looking down upon them, watching over them, granting wishes and answering their prayer requests…so long as they went to church every Sunday, dropped ten percent of their paycheck in the collection plate, and didn't get divorced or dance…or if they did, at least they had learned how to hide it from him.

For Eleanor, it was so much more than that. The simpletons around her may have chosen to disregard the dark energies, the demonic entities, the parallel universes and portals that constantly shifted all around them, but it certainly didn't make those things go away. Nor did it make their effects upon these non-believers' lives any less severe. They were constantly affected by them; yet remained in denial. They simply chose to ignore it all. But not Eleanor, she could see it. All of it. The things they couldn't explain, she sought the answers for. The ideals they shunned, she embraced. The ancient secrets they'd lost, she kept. She believed. She practiced.

In spite of all of this, Eleanor, like her husband, could see the value in keeping some things hidden from her daily life. After all, the secrets of the ancients weren't open for everyone, they were sacred. Closely held by a select group of individuals, wise women and men who knew their value. Knew their power. Knew not only how, but when to use them. So, she kept them all safely locked away. To any of her bridge-playing friends, the girls at the club, her minister, she was merely Eleanor Bond. Mayor's wife, and proud member of Hollingshead First Lutheran Church.

This morning began just like any other. At five in the morning Eleanor ventured to the kitchen to prepare her husband, Tilman, his favorite breakfast. They had a cook, but breakfast was never part of her charge, because only Eleanor knew just how her husband liked his eggs, and only she could prepare the bacon exactly as he wanted it. So this morning, like any other, she swam around the sea of marble and stainless steel that was her grand kitchen; grabbing a little of this and adding just a dash of that.

    Wrapped in her Italian silk night robe, atop fuzzy slippers, with her two stocky corgis: Felix and Oscar yapping at her heels, hoping she'd drop them a scrap of bacon, everything was perfectly routine. Only, today was different. Today was special. Sure, she always carefully flipped his fried eggs so that they didn't break, but today she made him three instead of his usual two. She added a few extra tablespoons of real maple syrup to his strips of bacon as they sizzled in the pan; the way she used to make it, before it was decided that he needed to cut back on the sugar. His black coffee was even more scalding than usual, and knowing that he always started with the Political Op-Eds of the paper, she made sure to have that section prominently waiting next to his coffee cup when he sat down in his chair at the head of the table. Little things that would butter him up; but not tip him off that she was working him up to ask a favor. A favor that she knew he wouldn't like. A favor that she knew she may well have to exercise that outspoken, assertiveness that she wasn't afraid to flex from time to time.

"The bacon's delicious this morning," he said through a half-chewed mouthful.

"You like it?"

"And three eggs? What did I do to deserve all this?"

He raised an eyebrow at her, playfully.

"I just like to take care of my husband."

She cupped his chin, turned his face toward hers, and planted a kiss on his greasy, wet lips. He smiled.

"I think you're just buttering me up for something. Either it's bad news or you're wanting something. Which is it?" he chuckled as he sipped his coffee.

Maybe he knew her a little better than she'd given him credit for.

"Alright, you've got me. There is something. I was hoping you could do something for me."

"I'm listening."

"Andie Sterling is in town..."

"Who?"

"The writer."

"I've never heard of her. What's she written?"

"Nothing that you've read, *I'm sure*."

"Oh, some of your ghost stories, eh?"

Tilman was a practical man. He thought any literary

work, involving fiction, was a waste of time. Even though he tolerated Nora's nightly reading in bed, he often told her that her time would be better spent falling asleep between the pages of some biography of a notable president, like Lincoln or Monroe. These *dime store novels* as he called them weren't worth the paper they were printed on.

"Tilman, I was hoping that you might be able to figure out where she's staying. I'd love the chance to meet her."

"Nora, you know I'd do anything for you, honestly, truly. But I really don't think that it's a good idea."

"Oh, you're just being stubborn. What harm could it do? She's a *writer*. One of my favorites. All I'm wanting is to grab a simple cup of coffee with her; maybe have her sign a book or two. What good is it to have a mayor for a husband if he isn't willing to pull a few strings every now and then?"

"My dear, why do you think she's here? Here of all places?"

"You're obsessed, Tilman, really…"

"Nora, the *Festival of Leaves* is coming up next month. You know how it draws in the tourists. It also means millions in revenue."

"Of course I do, what does that have to do with—"

"This town has worked hard to clean up its reputation.

But every once in a while one of these fiction writers comes around, poking their nose where it doesn't belong. Hoping to find a story that we don't want told."

"Tilman, that was years ago. What's the harm—"

"The harm is, we become a town with a *dark past*. A town that is *diseased*. The tourists stop coming, at least the ones who spend any money. Our economy dries up and we become a town of unemployed, meth addicts."

She laughed at this.

"Do you hear yourself? Don't you think you're being the least bit over dramatic?"

His face turned serious.

"Nora, honey, let's not forget that your family has ties to that past. Your own grandfather—"

"I know that, Tilman."

"*Well*, think about what would happen to all the charities you run. The organizations that you spearhead. If word were to get out that he—"

"Fine, Tilman," she paused for a moment. "*Fine*. If you're *that* serious about this, then, let's just forget the whole thing."

"It's for the best, my dear," he appealed.

For a moment she almost snapped back at him, but

then she stopped.

"Finish your breakfast," she said with a smile, wiping the bacon grease from his chin.

Sure, she could've pushed him. But she didn't. She knew he was right. Part of her didn't care about the dark history of the town or at the very least what folks might say about it; but part of her did. Her family did have blood on their hands, and keeping their story safely locked away was a part of their legacy that she'd vowed to help preserve; whether she liked it or not. Besides, she could take a trip to New York and meet Andie at some book signing any old time.

So she chose to stay quiet. She chose to let him win… *this time.* After Tilman's incident last year, his cardiologist had told him that it was time to limit fried foods…that meant finding healthier options for his daily breakfast. *Maybe some avocado toast.* She'd save her trump card for that argument.

Yeah, that's what she'd do.

CHAPTER 4

"In one point four miles, your destination is on the left," she mocked her GPS's computerized voice.

Of course, it wasn't, really. Andie didn't have to look at her phone; it hadn't updated its coordinates for the last two hours. It wasn't uncommon for the app to be spotty in such rural areas, but this was ridiculous. She could've asked for directions, but she wouldn't; she was like a man in that regard, stubborn with pride.

Then again, who could she ask anyway? She had left the town proper hours ago. Though occasional signs and landmarks confirmed she was still in Hollingshead, there wasn't a sign of life anywhere —just miles and miles of rocky Maine coastline.

It was the kind of landscape that a Stephen King novel would droll on and on about. *Perhaps deservedly so*, she thought. It was beautiful but in a treacherous sort of way. Smoky gray jagged rocks, interrupted by sporadic tufts of emerald grass, stretched as far as the eye could see. Beyond the shoreline, a boundless sea of sapphire waves washed to and fro, breaking like glass against the coast.

The narrow road wasn't paved but was coated by an ancient layer of tar and fine gravel. Wound like a mooring line tossed into the wind, it jarringly teetered on the edge of the precipice — too daring for the casual Sunday driver, but just the kind of white-knuckle challenge Andie lived for.

Perhaps the all-too-eminent danger of driving off a cliff was a good thing. The dull, gray sky and a distant lull of thunder could easily persuade one to nod off to sleep, were they not actively engaged in such a daring task. This could especially be the case today.

Andie hadn't slept well since her plane landed in Bangor almost a week ago. Things had only gotten worse the closer she got to her destination. Intense nightmares, coupled with sleep paralysis, had kept her from getting the rest she needed to be of sound mind. Despite the prolific skill she had for chasing down the details of any story, she could feel her senses growing weak.

Come on, Andrea. Focus. She reminded herself of all the times that she'd had to push through even more difficult challenges to finish a book. After all, she was a female writer in the male-dominated world of fiction horror. Deadlines, the sleaziness of self-promotion, constantly selling herself to her publisher-this wasn't her first rodeo; this was a dance she knew all too well. *Lack of sleep, that's nothing.* And the visions, they were just dreams. Vivid as they were, they were nothing to worry about, *were they?* But what about the marks on her arm? She remembered just how intensely she could feel the demons breathing on her skin, the repulsive stench of death on their breath, and the shooting pain as their teeth broke through the skin on her arm. It must've been those dreams, where she was trying to fight them off, that she accidentally scratched up her own arms. Yeah, that made sense. Except the sleep paralysis. She couldn't move when she saw them, *so how—*

The phone rang, interrupting her thoughts. She was so lost in her mind, so anxious about the possibilities and her diminishing ability to reconcile them, that she nearly screamed at the playful ditty of her own ringtone. *Get a hold of yourself*, she scolded. In an instant she regained her bearings, calmed her breathing, and answered.

"Hey, Max."

"Good mornin', how's it goin'?"

His voice was too chipper for eight o'clock, but then again, he was a morning person. Andie knew this. Thanks to the night they grabbed that drink after his dad's funeral — *one lousy drink* — and they wound up sleeping together. Maybe it was his weakened emotional state. She'd never seen him so vulnerable, and she both loved and hated him for it. Or, maybe it was four years of sexual tension that had built up between them. She couldn't decide. They hadn't discussed that in the aftermath. They hadn't even talked about the incident since it happened almost two months ago. Andie hadn't brought it up, and Max seemed to be playing it cool, so maybe it was just a fluke thing. At least Andie hoped so. After all, she'd vowed to keep it that way.

"What's it like?" he continued.

"I'm not there yet."

"Oh, *really*? Everything OK?"

"Yeah, I'm fine. It's just that I can't seem to find it. It's not where it was listed on the map. And of course, my GPS is a *freak-show* out here."

"Well shit. Is there someone you could ask?"

"Oh yeah, for sure…hold on, lemme just pull over and ask this tree. Or maybe this rock; ya know, after 4.6 billion years, I'm pretty sure he knows the area."

"Aha. Very funny."

He was used to her sarcasm.

"There's absolutely *nothing* out here," she yawned. "And I'm literally about to fall asleep. Haven't slept a wink since I got here."

"Really? Why not?"

He sounded genuinely concerned.

"Uh … the bed," she laughed. "Last time I book an *Airbnb* with no reviews."

Of course, the bed was perfectly fine, but she refused to tell him about the dreams. Even though he was in them. *Because he was in them*. She wouldn't. Despite the fact that he'd never brought up the night of his dad's funeral, he *had* acted differently towards Andie ever since. The once sarcastic banter they used to share, all of the playful low-blows, had now grown very one-sided. He was softer. He showed concern. At first, she thought it was because his father's death had made him sentimental; she hoped that's all it was. But now, she wasn't taking any chances.

"I shoulda gone with you," he said regretfully.

"No!" she snapped back a bit more firmly than she'd intended to. "I mean, you know how I get when I'm writing. I'll find any reason to procrastinate. It's better if I'm alone."

Just then, the thunder snapped so fiercely that the reverberations nearly shook the car off the road.

"Was that *thunder*?!"

"Yeah. It just started pouring out of nowhere," she couldn't even see the headlights at the end of her hood.

"OK, I'm gonna let you go so you can drive. Be careful. And please, *please* call me when you get there," he pleaded.

"OK, OK. I will," she hung up the phone without saying goodbye.

The thunder was cracking again and again, like an angry horseman's whip. The wind was howling and wedging its way between the car windows. Andie could've sworn she heard it say her name. It was completely dark now, and she was leaning over her steering wheel to find the road when she suddenly slammed on her brakes.

There was something directly in front of her car. What was it? Was it a person? If it was, it'd have to be an abnormally large person. Was it a sign? Maybe it was a large elk or a moose. Were they the same thing? Did they even exist in Maine? Her mind raced from one thought to the next.

Meanwhile, it just stood there. Whatever *it* was. Seemingly unfazed by the pouring rain, it didn't move — dark and mysterious, except for small traces of light reflected by her headlights. She honked the horn, but the thing wouldn't budge.

"Dammit!" she exhaled as she continued honking and flashing her lights.

Gathering her nerve, she grabbed her umbrella and hesitantly opened the car door. Rain came flooding in from overhead. She emerged, fighting to get the umbrella open in a futile effort to keep herself from getting drenched. As her feet touched the ground, the ground gave way and she sank into mud up to her shins.

"Are you fucking kidding me?!"

A gust of wind blasted past and instantly turned her umbrella inside out. In a fit of rage, she nearly threw the useless thing off the edge of the cliff, or what she assumed to be the edge. She couldn't see that far. She decided to keep it, just in case she needed to use it to fight off ... whatever was out there.

She could see it a little better from outside. It wasn't a person. What could it be? She squinted through the dense rain and timidly inched closer. With every small step she swung the mangled umbrella like a sword. The thing didn't seem to be frightened.

It wasn't until she was almost directly in front of it that she could tell what it was. She laughed at herself, embarrassed at her melodramatic performance. All of this to scare off a rock. Well, not just a rock. This was a mammoth boulder. A boulder! Right in the middle of the road. Or maybe she'd run off the road? Either way, she breathed a little easier now.

It was almost black against the backdrop of the charcoal sky. The dreadful thing loomed over her. It must've been more than seven feet tall. How had she not seen this before? Surely she'd been driving in circles for the last two hours. There was a patch of something on its surface, right at eye level. Subconsciously, Andie reached out and dug her fingers into the dense, wet moss and pulled a large chunk of it away. She could feel something underneath the growth on the rock's surface. It felt like something had been carved into it. A few more swipes and the moss was all gone. Then she rubbed the rainwater into the muddy residue and wiped it away. She could now run her fingers along the surface. They were carvings, she was certain of that now. They felt like letters, maybe? It was still impossible to see in the darkness.

She sprang back to her car and returned with her phone. Throwing her jacket up over her head, she leaned her forehead against the rock and made a canopy with the collar of her jacket to block the rain. In the light of her phone's flashlight, she was clearly able to see it. She was right; they were letters. Letters that formed words. Line by line, they gathered to form a strange poem. But what did it mean?

> SHROUDED IN DARKNESS
>
> SHE LIES IN WAIT
>
> LURING FOOLISH MEN
>
> TO TEMPT THEIR FATE
>
> FOR HER COFFERS FILLED
>
> WITH TREASURES UNTOLD
>
> BUT HASTEN THEIR ESCAPE
>
> LEST THEIR SOULS SHE SHOULD HOLD

"*Oh my God.*"

This is incredible, she thought. She tried to make sense of the words. Who carved this and when? She leaned back and tried to take a picture of it.

Another crack of thunder and lightning caught Andie

off guard, causing her to drop her phone. The phone hit the road with a crunch, casting shattered bits of it around the space at her feet. Andie pictured the grainy footage of the atomic bomb tests as she stood helpless to stop it from happening.

"Fuuuuuck!!!"

Her words were drowned out by another clap of thunder. With a heavy sigh, she retreated back to the driver's seat. There was nothing she could do now but wait out the storm.

As she settled back in, she peeled off her jacket and shook her drenched hair out like a dog getting out of the bathtub. Thick droplets of water flung about the car's interior as if they were blood spatters in a crime scene. *Good thing it's not cold,* she reassured herself. After locking the doors, she reclined her seat and kept repeating the words of the poem aloud. Why would someone carve such a thing into a rock in the middle of nowhere? Was it a sign? A sign that she was heading the right direction? Maybe. Unable to make sense of the whole thing, she broke down each line and tried her best to draw a conclusion as to its meaning. This worked to calm her nerves. As her heartbeat settled back down into a relaxed cadence and with the threat of driving off a cliff now safely behind her, Andie's eyes grew heavy and she succumbed to the now-gentle rolls of thunder, the soft tapping of the rain on the windshield. Within minutes she helplessly drifted off to sleep.

CHAPTER 5

Max hung up the phone. With a heavy sigh he further collapsed his frame into the expanse of the white leather office chair. Its chrome arms reflected the intense light of the morning sun; it was almost blinding. He thought it strange how it could be so bright and sunny in New York City, and storming so violently in Maine. The thunder sounded so loud on the other end of the phone. *Ugh, Maine.* He couldn't stop thinking about Maine. Sure, she'd be alright, he had no doubts. But he still wished that she had asked him to come along.

He cursed himself for not pushing for it when she was planning her trip. Why shouldn't she want him to come? After all, he had skin in this game too. If chasing down this story didn't result in a book, a book that sells, then Max would be the one taking the heat.

She'll call. She said she'd call. She did say that, right? He assured himself that he was just being paranoid. *If she said she'll call, she'll call.* Still, she'd been gone the better part of a week and she hadn't called him once. *Not once.* It was always him calling her.

Was he being obvious enough? Too obvious? Maybe. He'd been trying to lay low and keep things casual with Andie ever since they hooked up. *There was definitely something there, right?* He was damn sure there was. At least for him. As for Andie, he could only hope. *I'm not getting back at her when she takes a jab at me. I've eased up on her with deadlines.* Then he remembered how she said she'd only procrastinate if he were around. Maybe she thought he'd become too lenient on her. *Dammit!* But he was just trying to show concern and consideration for her. That's what women want. *That is what they want, isn't it?*

Unfortunately, Max's ideas about what women look for in a mate could be traced back to the small handful of Rom-Coms he'd seen over the years. And not even the good ones. While there may be some women out there looking to play the sweet damsel in distress, breathlessly awaiting their knight in shining armor to come and rescue them from their ivory tower, Andie sure as hell wasn't one of them. She'd just assume to reverse the roles and save the guy's ass, rather than to give him the satisfaction of thinking that she needed him. Deep down Max knew this. That didn't stop him from trying though. He'd show up to the office with coffee and she wouldn't say thank you. He'd open doors. He'd pull out chairs. He even made it a point to ask her opinion when the situation didn't really call for it. None of that had any effect. Even at thirty-two, Max had never loved anyone. He'd always been too wrapped up in becoming a lead editor for a prestigious publishing house; but somehow, realizing that dream, didn't hit quite the way he thought it would. Then along came Andie, and all that was shot to hell.

    He signed her after she'd been dropped by her previous publisher; only she didn't know she was going to be dropped. Her first book with them had been a runaway success and it was expected that her second would follow suit, but it didn't even come close. Back then she was green to the industry. A contact at her publisher had given Max her name, and he slipped his business card into a copy of her book at a *Barnes & Noble* book signing. When she opened up the cover and saw it, she looked up to see Maxwell Tate smiling back at her.

THE HAND THAT FEEDS YOU

To be fair, this is worth noting because it was a great smile. It was the kind of smile that often got him into meetings with high ranking executives-instead of just their low-level counterparts, or got him invited to be a guest speaker at industry events and major public appearances; it's what got him into his own high-rise corner office, working for *Beekman & Burghman Publishers* as Editor-in-Chief of their fiction department, and, more than he cared to admit, he would use it to get free drinks at bars and gas stations.

Andie just stared up at him. It wasn't really a question of whether or not she noticed the smile, she did, but she also saw through the bullshit. Max was gonna have to work harder than he was used to. See, ever since she was a little kid, Andie realized that she had an incredible bullshit meter. Some people are naturally athletic. Others can sing or dance. Andie could do two things really well...tell stories and see through bullshit.

"What am I supposed to do with this?" she asked, holding up his business card.

"It's got my info on it..."

"I can read," she said sarcastically. "In my line of work that's always a plus."

"I'd just like to talk."

"I've already got a publisher, what makes you think I want to talk to you?"

Just then Max felt a tap on his back. He turned around to find the culprit. It was a fat, middle-aged man, with a round scruffy face and curled lip-to help him breathe out of his mouth. His gut, a fleshy fanny-pack, was draped below his graphic T shirt and his baggy jeans looked like they had been made from several pairs-sewn together. *Maybe they were made to clothe an elephant,* thought Max.

"Come on, man! We're all waiting here!"

Max looked past him and saw a line of people; all of whom had similarly unpleasant expressions on their faces. Max gave a polite nod, and said,

"Almost finished."

He then turned back to Andie.

"I guess I'm waiting on you, too," she said.

Whether she was being serious, or playful, Max couldn't tell.

"Waiting?"

"For your answer. I told you I've already got a publisher, yet you're still here-insisting I wanna talk to you, and I wanna know why."

She folded her arms, and sat back in the chair. This

was a power pose for her. Her eyes were fixed, and serious, but the corners of her mouth were trying not to smile. Max could see this now. She was playing with him.

"Come on, buddy, let's go. Huh?!"

The fatty behind him was spouting off again. This time Max ignored him.

"I think your publisher is holding you back. I want you to have the freedom to make your own choices..."

She faked a yawn, and then called out to the line, "Next!"

"No, no, wait..." Max implored.

"Move it buddy, she said next. I'm gettin' tired of standin' here!"

The words came booming from behind him. Something in Max snapped, and this time he wasn't playing around.

"Listen fat-ass, why don't you go sit down and take a load off the floor, huh? I'm sure your knees and kankles will thank you for it!"

Without missing a beat he was back to staring at Andie, whose eyes were now bulging out of her head in disbelief.

"And as for you, Ms. Sterling, *true*, your first book

was a smash. But we both know this one is *a total shit-show!*"

He held up her book.

"Why is this, you ask?" Max went on, "well, my honest opinion is that it was a shoddy rush-job, with piss-poor editing, and not enough in the publicity budget to make anyone give two shits about it. Some of that may be your fault, but I think the majority of these problems lie with your lame-ass publisher, who doesn't realize what a gift they've been given just to have you on their roster. In fact the *only* reason that I'm buying a copy of this hideous Lovecraft wannabe is so we can look back on it a year or two from now, when you've got a string of *Pulitzers* behind your name, and we can joke about how you wasted the first three years of your writing career at some *do-nothing* publishing house!"

He was breathing like an overweight, hellfire and brimstone preacher from Alabama, at a summer tent revival.

"Uh, with...me...at my firm. I was supposed to mention that in all of...of that."

His explosion of confidence was running out of him like antifreeze in a cracked radiator. She just sat there, staring up at him. Everyone was quiet now; stunned by his profanity-laden outburst. He'd even impressed himself-at least while he was in the moment. Now he wasn't sure what to think.

Without a word, her eyes went down to the blank white page of the book's inside cover. She signed it, and handed it up to him. She still wasn't showing her hand.

What the hell was she thinking?

"Thank you."

He folded the book under his arm, which was now closer to a broken wing. After a quick passing glance at the queue behind him, he dropped his eyes to avoid any more eye contact, tucked his tail, and proceeded to walk away. And then, just when he least expected it,

"Mr Tate!"

He looked back.

"...I'll call you," the corners of her mouth drew back into that thin smile, and she went back to signing books.

That was four years ago. Four incredible years. Andie wasn't just some fledgling author with one lucky title to her name, she was a *New York Times Bestseller*, several times over. She was in demand. Max hadn't *discovered* her, but he had given her everything that he had promised; and that, was freedom. Over the years they'd grown to be close friends, which worked surprisingly well in both their personal and professional relationships. For the first few years, that was fine with Max. He'd never seen Andie as anything more than a talented writer and a good friend. They shared the same sarcastic sense of humor. He knew what she liked in her coffee. And when she sent him a manuscript that didn't live up to what she was capable of, he'd call her out on it; and she was grateful for it.

So when did it all change? It wasn't just *that* night; when they'd hooked-up. That may have been when things finally came to a head, no pun intended, but the wheels were set in motion long before then. *But when?* Max couldn't think of the moment when it happened; it just happened.

Like, you wake up one day and there's this person that you see every single day, but suddenly, you see them in a way you've never seen them before. If Andie felt anything towards him, she wasn't saying anything. Like any typical guy, the thrill of the chase made him want her that much more. She was all he could think about, and he was willing to do whatever it would take, for just a chance with her.

But for now, that meant he had to play the game. He'd give her space, keep dropping subtle hints, and wait. Waiting was the worst. He hated the waiting. The next few minutes he'd spend tapping his phone screen, just to see it light up; just to see it say, *No New Calls*.

Until…

THE HAND THAT FEEDS YOU

Ring. Ring.

The screen lit up and his fumbling hands almost dropped the damn thing. Then his heart sank when he read who was calling.

"Hey Ray," he tried his best to hide his disappointment.

"My man, how ya doin' Maximilian?"

"You know, just living the dream, hashtag blessed, and all that bullshit."

"Haha! I feel ya man, I feel ya."

"So what's up?"

Max didn't return the *how are you* pleasantries because given the chance, Ray could talk for hours. Best to steer the conversation to business with him. Keep him on task.

"Well I got some info on that story up in Maine."

"Oh, no way! I thought you'd come up empty-handed."

"C'mon *M&M*, you know ya boy Ray always gets the goods!"

Max hated when Ray called him that, almost as much as he hated Maximilian.

"What ya got for me?"

"It's a lot to cover over the phone, why don't we meet up for coffee in an hour or so? I know there's a local shop on the same block as your office."

"Why can't you just tell me now? Email what you've got and we'll discuss it over the phone."

"No can do," Ray was playing hardball. "This shit ain't even on the internet. I had to pull quite a few strings to get it. Trust me brother, you'll want to hear it. One hour, *cool*?"

Shit. "Sure man, one hour."

*****

"I'll take a *Venti Americano*, please."

The barista frowned. Max had even flashed his smile. *What the heck?*

"Sir we don't have *Venti* sizes here," she sounded offended that he'd even say such a word.

Might as well have dropped the F-bomb, he thought. Unfortunately this last thought came somewhat out-loud.

"Ffff-ine. I'll take a large, I guess."

It was a sloppy recovery. He tried the smile thing again. No luck. *Was this thing on?* The barista rolled her eyes and grabbed the cash from his hand as if it were her intention to rip the money in two. *Geez, lady, if you hate it so much why are you even here?* Though he could just as easily ask himself the same question.

It was Friday. Fridays are always a pain in the ass. Friday means tomorrow is Saturday, which means the printers are closed-at least they're not answering phones or responding to emails. This means if his office has an order of ten thousand titles coming off the press and he discovers that some junior proofreader missed an error, the publishing company will either be sending out ten thousand books with a typo or his ass will be responsible for the costs of the damages. At that point you pray the typo is minor and no one will care enough to raise any fuss. Not like some early versions of the *King James Bible* that said "*children should be killed*" instead of "*filled*," or how it talks about "*God's great ass*" instead of "*greatness.*" Good thing nothing quite that bad had ever slipped by on his watch.

"Maxine! Over here!"

Max grabbed his coffee and looked around to see Ray seated at a small two-top, waving his arms like a giant bird. *Why can't the sonofabitch just pick one annoying nickname and stick with it?*

Ray was in his late twenties, and Max had known him since he was a teenager. They met at *Duke* when Max found himself re-taking a freshman computer class because of an error on his high school transcript. It was a class that was supposed to carry over, but didn't. Even back then Ray couldn't stop talking. Too afraid to blow off the computer class, and risk failing, Max worked out a deal with Ray. In exchange for Ray doing all of his homework for the computer class, Max would write papers for Ray's English Comp class. Ray's English grade improved, Max had more time to focus on the classes he needed to graduate; it was a win-win. All these years later, they still had a working relationship. Max would pay Ray to dig up info on the deep web, or basically anywhere. If the information existed, Ray was the guy to find it. Despite the awful nicknames and the rambling stories, *Ray was a valuable asset*, Max reminded himself as he approached the table.

"Hey Ray, whatcha got for me?"

Not even gonna give him the chance to start—

"Got the *Americano* I see. I was in the mood for somethin' cold, myself…"

Damn, it didn't work.

"Nice. So, you got somethin' for me, or what?"

"Always business with you," Ray joked. "Yeah, bro, I got it."

THE HAND THAT FEEDS YOU

Ray's eyes sparked with excitement, as he pulled out a tattered notebook. This thing had obviously seen some love. *Or maybe abuse?* Sharing his findings was something Ray always delighted in. Think of an Olympic gold medalist taking their victory lap-in front of a stadium of thousands of cheering fans; that was Ray in this moment.

"So," Ray began, "this place in Maine, Hollingshead, it's become known for its number of disappearances over the years. Thirteen in the last hundred, to be exact. All men. All were last seen heading up to the coastline a couple miles outside of the town. None of them were ever found—"

"Suicides."

"Excuse me?"

Ray shot him the same look a teacher does, when you give the wrong answer in class.

"Well, that *would* be the obvious explanation, right? I mean a handful of people living in an area that's known for being dreary and depressing, throw themselves into the sea. Happens in the Pacific Northwest all the time. These are all facts we already knew."

Max was spearheading here. He did that occasionally. It wasn't intentional; he was just very factual and detail-oriented. While it made for a good editor, it often made him a lousy sport when playing games of *Trivial Pursuit*, or on days like this.

"Ya finished? You...you want me to continue?" Ray was through with having the wind taken out of his sails.

Max threw up his hands in apologetic surrender. He knew when he was being called out for being an asshole.

"My bad. *Sorry.*"

"As I *was saying*," Ray continued, "*you already know* about the thirteen men who have disappeared there. What you *don't* know is that there are actually far more than that."

He flipped open the cover of his notebook-revealing a full page of chicken scratch that Max couldn't read; at least not upside down.

"One hundred and fifty seven, that I could confirm," Ray said.

Max shook his head as his brain gave an instant replay of the statistic.

"And," Ray went on, "just like those thirteen unlucky bastards, these were all men. And not a single body found."

Ray relished in having the upper-hand. He had Max hanging on now, so he threw a little theatrics into his performance. His delivery became something like Vincent Price, *or maybe Hitchcock* is who he was thinking of. *Eh, you know what they say, all white guys look the same.*

"Wait, wait," Max threw up a hand. He was still trying to process. "So, you're saying a hundred and fifty men went missing—"

"A hundred and fifty seven."

"A hundred and fifty seven, *right*. And only thirteen were reported? How is that *possible*?"

"Aww, man you're makin' me feel smart. I figured this out faster than you are. And you're always Mr. Smart Guy."

When Ray had a good laugh, like one of those deep belly laughs, his entire mouth would draw back in a way that all of his teeth were forced outside of his head. Max thought they looked like prisoners making a mass-escape. He wished someone would call the guards and beat them into submission. Or maybe it was closer to the cowcatcher of some old steam train as it headed West. Either way, Max was through with being made fun of.

"What's your point?" he snapped, childishly.

Ray settled back down.

"OK, OK. Think about it. A hundred and fifty seven. Out of a town of less than two thousand. And these were all men-which men make up sixty percent of the town's population, so we could take that population down to less than a thousand."

"*OK?*" Max still wasn't getting it.

"They weren't all from *Hollingshead*."

Max felt like an idiot. It was obvious to him now. And Ray was the one to point it out to him. That made him feel even worse. Nothing against Ray, but for the first time Max wondered if all of the time he spent chasing after Andie was causing him to slip. Ray kept going.

"In fact, only the thirteen were. The rest weren't documented because—"

"Because they came there from *somewhere else*!" Max was firing on all cylinders now.

"...right."

"And no one thought to connect the dots because these men came from all over! They had no connection to one another..!" Max almost got a hard-on from being *so* right.

"You're doing it *again*," Ray moaned.

"Sorry, this is just, oh my god, this opens up so many possibilities. How did you find this out?"

"You really think I'm gonna give you my sources?" Ray cocked his head to the side and raised one eyebrow.

"Touché."

This was all Max needed to go on. Andie wasn't out there chasing dead ends. There *was* a story out there. He was so happy he almost hugged Ray. *Almost.*

"You owe me one," Ray was starting his victory lap again.

"You got it, man. Next time...I've gotta make a call."

Max playfully double-tapped his fist on the table to keep from squealing like a schoolgirl.

"I'll catch ya later, thanks Ray!"

And with that, Max grabbed his coffee, and he was gone.

Ray threw his head back, smiled, and closed his eyes. The crowd was cheering his name now.

This was his moment.

*****

Max looked at his phone. *She still hasn't called.* He paced the sidewalk in front of the coffee shop for a solid minute. Should he call? Should he wait for her to call? *She said she would—alright Max, enough with your bullshit.* He had a job, and part of his job was to give his writers everything they need to succeed. This was relevant information. *Andie needs this information. It's not for me. It's for her,* he justified. With hands shaking, he called her number.

The phone rang twice, then,

"Hi, this is Andie. Sorry I missed your—"

Shit!

He hung up the phone. In an instant he knew what he would do. Within an hour he was at the airport, carrying an overnight bag, and a one way ticket for Bangor Maine.

CHAPTER 6

The room was round. There was a flagstone floor and field-stone walls. Floating timbered beams stretched across the lonely expanse overhead. A fire roared within the carved stone fireplace-that took up nearly the entire wall against which it sat. Both the firebox and hearth were painted with a smattering of soot. Across the room, a great glass window served as a reminder of the outside world. Everything looked small from up here. Whoever dwelt in this room wasn't a prisoner, but everything served to remind them that they didn't belong.

The furnishings were just as cold and unwelcoming as the chamber. A small bed tucked itself in the corner-positioned for a clear view of the door across the room. In the center of the room, atop an heirloom Persian rug, a splintering table sat next to a dusty velvet chair. In this chair, there was a woman.

 If anyone could look as though they belonged to this room, she did. Her pale skin was not white, but rather, it seemed to have no color at all. Likewise, there was no color on her lips. In fact, the only color upon her face could be found in her deep chestnut eyes, which were wrapped in an envelope of thick black lashes and sealed with a pair of strong mahogany eyelids. There was a time that she'd worn makeup, but now, that was not allowed. Nearly everything about her seemed to be devoid of color. Her midnight hair was drawn into a bun on the back of her head. It was pulled so tightly that she could feel it sliding back and forth each time she blinked her eyes. She wore a long black dress, which flowed from the floor to a high collar, and cinched around her neck. Her head seemed as if it were perching, or merely floating above her body.

 She was reading from an old book. The book was unfitting for this room. Unfitting for this *woman*. Its cover was thick and garishly lavish. The portrait of a king was proudly displayed at the center, and he was surrounded by small rubies and pearls; emeralds and amber. Her long, bony finger turned the yellowed page. The script was an ancient

Romanian dialect-this she read aloud.

The little girl was blonde. She was a pretty thing, wrapped in billows of pale pink chiffon. Her golden ringlets, which were loosely tucked into a pink ribbon, tossed about like ocean waves as she moved her head. If the woman in black thought *she* didn't belong here, this child definitely did not belong *here*.

She stood on her tiptoes, to spy on the scene below. The great, green lawn seemed to glow when it was touched by the warm sunbeams that peaked through the delicate folds of sullen clouds. This wasn't what she was watching though. It was the swarm of people. The busy worker bees. Dozens of servants, dressed in white from head to toe, were setting up for a lavish party. At the center of them was the lady of the house. Her arms were sweeping this way and that, telling the servants where to put the gifts, and how to arrange the flowers. Everything had to be perfectly so. *Everything*. The girl could almost hear her barking at them from the lonely tower.

"And what happened next?" the child was still gazing out the window.

"Would you like to see it?" the woman's Wallachian accent was brute and strong.

She patted a vacant knee, beckoning the girl to come join her.

The girl nestled into a comfortable position as the woman drew an arm around her, and gently stroked her sunny hair.

"The king invited all of the men to a grand party."

"Like today?" the girl asked.

"Yes. I suppose it may have been something like that," the woman said softly.

"Was it a birthday party?"

"No, my dear," she chuckled. "This was very different than a birthday party."

Another page turned-revealing a vibrant watercolor. It showed a medieval castle, engulfed in flames.

"There was a fire?"

"Yes. After everyone had eaten, the king ordered the castle doors to be locked. Then he had the castle set on fire."

"What happened to the people? Did they die?"

"Yes."

"Why? Why would the king do that?"

There wasn't a hint of trepidation in the girl's question; rather, it was filled with insatiable curiosity.

"The men were a threat to the kingdom. The king did

this because the men were standing between him and his people."

"So, he killed them."

This wasn't a question, the girl was merely vocalizing what she was internally rationalizing.

"Sometimes we must do unpleasant things, in order to do great things," the woman whispered gently.

The door flew open and crashed against the wall. The lady of the house came sweeping into the room. There was a stern expression on her face and her cheeks were flushed with anger. As she stood there, she shined like a beacon in stark contrast to the dreadful space in which she stood. Her dress was made of dazzling spun silk-in varied shades of green and blue. To the girl she looked like a peacock-even more so due to the lush feathers-sprouting from her Gibson hair.

"*Isabella*! I have been looking all over for you! What are you doing up here?!"

She threw out a hand for the girl to come.

"We were just reading, momma."

Though the girl called her *mother*, she felt nothing towards her.

"I told you not to read this blasphemous garbage to her!"

The mother grabbed the book and threw it into the fire.

"No!" the woman sprang to her feet.

"They're just stories," cried the girl.

"They are *not* just stories. They are *dangerous*," the mother protested.

"You're right. They're not just stories..." the woman said in a low tone. "They're a part of history. *Her* history..."

Her smile was menacing, as she locked eyes with the mother. There was something dangerous about her gaze. It was almost hypnotic. The mother felt as if she were falling into a trance.

"Bella go downstairs," the mother was insistent.

"But I don't want—"

"Now!"

The girl looked up at the woman.

"It's OK, Doniă..." the woman assured her.

"Do not call her that!" the mother was up in her face now.

"Why not? It's her name," the devious smile returned.

"It is *not* her name," the mother's eyes blazed with fury.

In one fell swoop, Bella's mother took her by the arm

and whisked her into the hall.

"Downstairs. *Now*," she ordered.

Then she slammed the door, leaving the girl on one side; herself and the woman on the other. The mother drew a few deep breaths. Then...

"They are *not* just stories. They are her *heritage*," the woman was resolute.

"You had no right..."

"I cannot stand by and watch—"

"No right!" the mother struck the woman's face.

Outside the door, the girl lay her ear next to the crack at the floor, so she could listen to the conversation inside.

"What *else* have you told her?"

The woman said nothing. Her gaze became intense once more.

"We had an agreement, *Camilla*. Do you remember?" asked the mother.

Silence.

"We allowed you to come with us. Allowed you work for us so you could watch her grow."

"I am just your filthy servant! Don't make yourself out to be some saint," Camilla's teeth were clinched.

"You would not have survived the revolution. Once

they found out you had ties to this family—"

"At least I would have died with some dignity! Look at *you*! You've forgotten *everything*. And now you're keeping it all from *her*. She has the right to *know*...she deserves to know the *truth*!"

"Her father and I will decide what's best for her," the mother condescended.

"I carried her in my womb for nine—"

"Carrying a child in your womb does not make you a mother."

"*Neither* does *buying* a child," Camilla said.

Belinda stood there. Angry, but unable to counter the attack. Camilla was right. Having been born into a world of privilege, Belinda may have been dealt a more favorable hand in life; but this woman could do something that she couldn't. And that, was to bear children.

*****

There was a sea of pink. Pink silk, pink flowers, pink toile. There were pink ponies, pink gifts wrapped in pink bows. Everywhere you looked, more pink. Except for the guests. And, of course, the servants. And even Bella's parents. No one was allowed to wear pink, except for the birthday girl. This was her party, and no one would be able to upstage her.

    Situated high upon the cliff, the great lawn overlooked the coast. The lush green grass lay like soft carpeting, and it seemed to stretch for miles. There were no trees on this side of the house, however the lawn was lined with perfectly manicured shrubs-many of which had been sculpted into fantastic animal-like shapes.

    Ornately carved stone steps, bedecked with sweeping stone balusters, delicately tethered the great lawn to a splendid mansion. High in the lonely tower of the house, Camilla watched, like a ghost.

    Bella cared very little for the party. While there were a few dozen children her age in attendance, she didn't know them. And she didn't like them. They were the children of her parents' friends. This party was more for her parents than it was for her. Even at seven years old, she knew enough to know where she ranked in their world. The parents cared about money and maintaining their place in high society. This party was merely one more way to flaunt their wealth in hopes of making their friends jealous.

    "Happy birthday, darling!" Carlisle initiated a round of applause as two servants appeared, carrying a large cake.

    The ridiculous thing stood at least three feet tall.

"It's white," said the girl.

"Not now, Bella," Belinda appealed.

"But I wanted a pink cake! I told you that! I want a *pink* cake!"

The girl was making a scene. The guests looked at her parents, waiting for them to intervene.

Belinda pulled her daughter aside.

"This is not the time, nor the place. You have guests."

"They're not my guests, they're *your* guests!"

"What's gotten into you?"

The mother was losing her patience.

"I told you the only thing I wanted was a pink cake. I told you..." the girl cried.

"I know that, but we needed something to balance out all of the pink. Besides, a pink cake would have been *too gauche*."

"I hate you!" the girl screamed, as she bolted for the house.

"Bella! Come back here! *Darling?*" Belinda was pleading, while trying to remain in character for her guests.

Just then a clap of thunder jolted from across the sea. In an instant the dark skies opened up and a cascade of rain came sweeping across the lawn. The women were screaming as their piles of coiffed hair broke into a stringy mess. The giant birthday cake slid off the stretcher and landed in a heap on the ground. The children ran around screaming in delight.

"Everyone inside! We'll move the party inside...we have plenty of room *inside!*"

The lady of the house was determined to end the affair on a high note.

As the guests settled themselves into the ballroom, they sipped tea, or warmed themselves by the roaring fire. The servants scrambled to find every blanket they could to keep the guests comfortable while they waited out the storm. The kitchen staff was busy making food out of the ingredients they had leftover.

All the while the girl's mother was weaving through the room, mingling with the guests-trying her best to put a positive spin on the afternoon. She was all smiles until one of the servants approached her and whispered,

"Ma'am you'll want to come see this."

In the far, dark corner of the room, Camilla was seated in a chair-with Bella sitting on her lap. The girl was eating a small slice of cake with pink frosting.

"What are *you* doing here?!"

"Doniă invited me," said Camilla.

"You are *not* welcome here. Get out!"

"She made me a pink cake," Bella said, accusingly.

"I knew she wanted one, so I thought I might surprise her. I hope you don't mind."

Belinda took the plate from the girl's hands.

"Give that back, it's *mine*!"

"I said get out! And take this hideous mess with you."

She shoved the plate into the woman's hands. Camilla stared at it, then said,

"You know nothing about raising a child. She is not happy here with you. She told me so."

"You've turned her against us," the mother cried.

"*Have I?*"

"You've poisoned her mind with those ridiculous stories…"

"You cannot force a child to love you. You cannot force them to choose you—"

"Get *out*…"

"I believe she's ready to make her choice. Why don't we let her choose, *huh*?"

She knelt down to the girl.

"What do you say, Doniă? Which would *you* choose?"

Before the girl could respond,

THE HAND THAT FEEDS YOU

"I said get the *hell* out of my house!"

The mother slapped the woman across the face.

The room stood still. All eyes were on them now. Camilla took a few breaths to keep herself from striking back, then,

"*Fine*. I'll go. But you cannot force her to choose you *forever*. Just like you cannot force her father to choose you. To *love* you. One day they will make their own choices. And when that day comes, you'll either learn to live with the consequences…or you will *die* because of them."

She caressed the girl's face and looked into her eyes one last time.

"Goodbye my Doniă."

The girl had tears streaming down her cheeks. Her rosy face was trapping the waves of fury that were raging just below the surface.

✶✶✶✶✶

Camilla didn't turn around until she reached the road. *I won't look back,* she had promised herself…but she knew she had to. One last look, before it was all gone, forever. The man that she loved, who hadn't been man enough to keep his promise to choose *her*. The child whom she called her own. Just one last look before she let them go, *forever*. Before it was all nothing more than just a sad memory.

From here the house was invisible. It seemed impossible that such a massive estate lie waiting-just beyond the rugged fortress of pines trees. Then her nose detected something. *Was that smoke?* A thin stream of smoke rose gently above the thick blanket of treetops. *Oh no. No!*

She ran back up the long road, towards the house, as fast as her legs could carry her. Her heartbeat raced wildly. The air was getting heavier. It was getting hotter; much hotter. Black smoke was everywhere now, and she could smell more than just burning wood. *Was that...? It was. Burning flesh.*

"Doniă! Carlisle!!!"

She stopped dead in her tracks when she saw the girl standing in front of her-waiting. She scooped the girl up in her arms and kissed her again and again.

"Donia, it's alright. I'm here."

Flames were bursting out of every window as the house became engulfed in the blaze.

"Where is everyone?" the woman asked.

And that's when she heard it. The wailing. The screaming. Blood-curdling screams. Hundreds of them. The resounding echoes of horror and pain. Women, children, she could hear all of them. All of them.

The girl stared up at the blaze. Then looked back to the woman.

"It's alright. Everything's going to be alright now. I choose you," she said.

"Oh, Doniă. What have you done?"

The woman looked up in horror. Then, thinking aloud, as if asking herself,

What have you done?

CHAPTER 7

"No!" Max flung forward in his seat-smacking his face on the seat-back in front of him. If he hadn't been wearing his seat belt, he'd probably have wound up in the lap of the guy next to him.

"Oh my god!"

"Sir are you alright?"

Several passengers left their seats to try and help.

"Ladies and gentlemen please return to your seats. Let's give him some room to breathe," said the flight attendant. "You OK, sir?"

"There was a fire."

Max was still out of breath.

"A fire? On the plane?!"

Someone started to panic.

"*No*, there's no fire on the plane. Ladies and gentlemen, I'm going to ask you again to take your seats. *Thank you*!"

The flight attendant was being curt with them now. Then he turned his attention back to Max.

"It was all just a dream, sir. Everything's gonna be OK," he said, warmly.

Max buried his face in his hands.

"But it felt so real. I...I could feel the heat of it...and I could hear them. I could hear them all. They were trapped, and I couldn't help them. I could see them, but I couldn't help them."

He was sobbing now.

Part of him felt like an idiot because a flight attendant was wiping away his tears with a hot towel, that and he'd also gotten some snot on the sleeve of the guy sitting in *4B*. But the other part of him didn't care.

Obviously it was all just a dream, but where did this come from? He didn't recognize any of the faces. This didn't stem from some scary movie he'd watched; at least none that he could remember. It was more like he was looking through a window into another world, watching this all play out, and then he was there. It felt real.

It was real.

It couldn't be real.

"I'll bet it was the sleeping pill that you washed down with the vodka from the minibar," said *4B*.

"Maybe," Max said.

But it wasn't. Max always took a pill with a little alcohol on a flight. He hated flying; and he flew a lot. He'd either wind up nauseous, puking his guts out in the airplane toilet, *which sucked*, or he'd be groggy for the rest of the day, *which sucked slightly less*. Nightmares were never part of the equation. *Never.*

✺✺✺✺✺

About four hundred miles away, in the driver's seat of a rental car, Andie was also dreaming.

"Andie...aaaaannndddiiee,"

She opened her eyes. The whisper came again,

"Aaaaannndddiiee."

She was still dreaming, and she knew it. She knew the feeling, and, this time, she was ready. Despite the nightmares, nightmares weren't something new to Andie.

When she was just a kid, she suffered from chronic night terrors and sleep paralysis. This went undiagnosed for awhile because Andie's parents thought she was just acting out for attention, but of course she wasn't. When she was eleven, her parents sent her away to a juvenile psychiatric hospital, where she'd spend a year undergoing psychoanalysis and daily counseling. She never forgave them for sticking her in there.

If there was one good thing that came from her time spent in the hospital; it was that someone finally took her claims seriously. A doctor worked with her to navigate her dreams. Over time she developed the ability to lucid dream. This helped her to be able to face her fears. To fight them when she could. To run when she couldn't. *"There's always an escape,"* her doctor would tell her. This all seemed to work. By the time she was cleared to go back home, the nightmares had stopped. She hadn't had one since. At least not until a week ago.

She drew in a deep breath and held it. *Seven, eight, nine, pfffffffff.* And again. Breathe in for five, hold it for five, let it out slowly, and all the way out on ten. She was a little out of practice, but it was coming back to her.

OK, now take in your surroundings. What do you see? She was in her car. Still in the driver's seat, and the seat was reclined. The sky was dark, it must've been nighttime now.

There was a full moon, and lots of stars. *OK, good. Don't forget to breathe. Keep breathing.* Until now she had only moved her eyes, while working to keep her head and body perfectly still. She felt safe enough to sit up.

She sat up and adjusted the seat to the upright position. The car was still in the same spot, with the giant rock positioned directly in front of her. She scanned the view from each window. There was nothing outside. Nothing out of the ordinary. A few more deep breaths, then she silently opened the door and climbed out.

The night air was cold. She could feel it tingling her skin. Goosebumps chased up her arms and down her back. She breathed the cold air in deeply. She breathed it in until it hurt. There had to be some reason she was here in this dream. She was ready to face it; whatever it may be.

The rock seemed to move. To dance in the moonlight. At first Andie thought it was just her eyes playing tricks on her, then she remembered this was a dream. *Stay skeptical, Andie. Trust nothing.* She kept her eyes fixed to the rock. Her intuition told her that while she was watching it, it was the thing that was watching her.

At first it was just a vibration, then, a pulse along the perimeter. And finally, like the stroke of an artist's brush, a murky black shadow swept across the rock and wisped in front of her.

"Andie..." the shadow whispered her name.

"What do you want from me?"

"Come here, Andie..."

The shadow was moving further away.

"Who are you?!" Andie demanded.

"I've been waiting for you...we've been waiting..."

"Tell me who you are!"

Andie was trying to control it, but she must've been too rusty. The shadow floated toward the edge of the cliff, then disappeared into the darkness. Andie knew it wasn't gone. She wasn't that stupid.

"Come back here! I demand to know who you are!"

After a few moments of silence, the dark form of a woman stepped out from the shadows. Andie couldn't make out a face, or any features. The form continued walking closer to the edge-where she stopped and looked out over the sea.

Andie couldn't explain why she felt this way, but she wanted to cry. An extreme wave of pain and sadness washed over her. She felt deep pain for this woman...for *this thing*. Her eyes began to burn, then her nose, and before she could stop them she could feel the salty tears welling up in her eyes.

This made absolutely no sense.

"Hello?"

The thing didn't look back.

"Is there a reason I'm here? Please, just tell me. *Please*."

Andie was weeping now. She had this strong desire to run to the thing and hug it-with every ounce of strength she had. She felt its sadness, its pain.

She didn't even realize that she'd started walking toward it…not until she was running. It didn't move away from the edge. Andie didn't know if it had its back or its face to her, she still couldn't see a face-if there was one.

When she was about a foot away, she stopped. It knew she was there. It had been waiting for her. There was something it wanted to tell her. Andie didn't say anything, she just waited. Then came a faint, disembodied whisper.

"What?" Andie asked, equally as quiet.

The thing whispered again. Still Andie couldn't make it out. With trembling hands, she reached out to touch it on the shoulder.

"What did you say?"

In an instant the thing spun around to face her, but just before she could see its face she heard it say,

"Open your eyes!"

★★★★★

Andie woke up face to face with the demon. The same demon she'd seen in her nightmares every night for the last week. It was sniffing her hair. If there was any flesh left on its face, she couldn't see it. It looked mostly like the vacant skull of a decomposed corpse, only different.

Much different.

The teeth were like sharp fangs. Not just the canines, all of them. Its dislocated jaw swung freely on its hinges, releasing a forked tongue. Once again, her stomach turned at the vile smell of its putrid breath. The tongue lapped at her cheeks like a friendly dog.

If only this were a dog.

It raised a limb, displaying its three-pronged claw. Her eyes followed its reach as it flew over her face and up to her head. Then she could feel it playing with her hair.

She tried to move. She tried to scream. She tried to breathe. No matter how hard she tossed and turned about internally, her body lay deadly still. Her heart was beating so furiously that she could not only hear it, but could feel the blood pulsing.

Come on. Come on! This isn't real. This isn't real!!!

Her chest was hurting from the lack of oxygen. *Breathe, dammit, breathe!!!* No matter how forcefully her mind would say the words, her body refused to cooperate. She kept watching the thing as it was watching her. She looked into the deep abyss of its eyes. She could see nothing in them. She wondered what it could see in her.

Her limbs were growing cold now. Her fingers and toes were numb. *You have got to breathe!* In that moment, she knew she only had one shot. If she didn't breathe soon, she'd never breathe again. Andie closed her eyes, and on the count of three she was going to give everything she had to get herself up.

OK Andie, you've got this. One…

Two…

Three!

Although it felt like she had pushed the weight of the world off her shoulders, Andie merely rolled over halfway into the passenger seat. Luckily, that was more than enough.

She drew in a gasp like never before, and when she was done, she gasped again; and again. This breathing felt amazing. It was like sex. Only better. Maybe not any other time, but in this moment, it sure as hell was better than any sex she'd ever had.

CHAPTER 8

Thwack, thwack, thwack! A loud pounding came on the outside of the car's window. Andie's relief quickly faded into panic. Someone or something was still out there, and it was trying to get in. She could see the outline of one, or maybe two, but little more. All around her, every square inch of window was covered in a thick layer of condensation. Andie felt like a fish, trapped in a murky fishbowl. The pounding came again.

"Who's there?" Andie tried to say.

But after all of the screaming in the cold night air, her voice only managed a raspy whisper.

Thwack, thwack, thwack!

Andie drew in a deep breath, then let it out. It was time to see what was out there, after all, she'd already faced one demon today, what's one more? She wrapped her trembling hand in a coat sleeve, then reached out to wipe the window.

Oh, thank god, it's just Bennett.

She saw his friendly, perfect white smile, beaming back at her. Andie let out a sigh of relief, then turned the key one click and rolled down the window.

"I thought this was your car. Everything alright?" he asked. His tone sounded more like a concerned father than an otherwise perfect stranger.

"Yes, I'm fine. I got caught in the storm."

"That's what Julia thought when you didn't come home last night. She sent us up here to look for ya."

He proudly pulled Jordan closer to the car window. Jordan smiled shyly and gave a quick wave, to which Andie returned.

"Nice to see you again, Jordan."

He blushed, but said nothing.

"Thank you, both," she continued. "It really was sweet of you to come all the way up here just to make sure I was alright."

"With the storms we have up here, you can never be too careful," Bennett insisted.

Andie nodded. After last night, she could certainly vouch for that.

"Well, thanks again, and thank Julia for me. You can head on back. I won't be far behind you."

"Afraid you ain't goin' nowhere like that. You might wanna take a look," Bennett pointed a finger and made a sweeping gesture to Andie's car.

Ugh great. There goes the deposit.

Andie opened the door and stepped out of the car.

"Yes sir, she's in there pretty good," Bennett laughed.

Apparently Andie *had* driven off the road, and now all four tires were buried in mud, all the way to the underside of the car.

"Perfect," she groaned.

"Ah, not to worry, my boy and I, we can getcha outta there, no problem."

He sent Jordan to grab the chains from their truck.

"You will be careful, won't you? This is a rental."

"No worries, done this a million times. Shouldn't take more than five or ten minutes," he said, reassuringly.

Now that she was standing, all of the liquid in her body had rushed down to crowd her bladder, and she suddenly couldn't resist the urge to pee.

"If you two will excuse me, nature is calling, or make that screaming," she said with an awkward laugh; then grabbed a handful of napkins from the glove compartment.

Thank goodness I hit that drive thru. She shuddered at the thought of having to use leaves as toilet paper. Knowing her luck, she'd accidentally opt for poison ivy or something. *Although, an itchy hoo ha would be the way to top off this perfectly awful trip.*

"Take your time, we'll honk when we getcha out," Bennett said.

Andie left them to it, and turned to the woods, in order to find some privacy.

After she'd walked about twenty yards or so, she stopped.

This seems far enough.

Even though she figured it was probably less than a hundred feet to the edge of the forest, she could no longer see the outside world. All around her there was nothing but trees. Ancient by the size of them. They towered over, so thick that they cut out almost all sunlight. Although the morning had been clear and the sun had been shining so bright, she was now standing in near total darkness.

After finishing the unpleasant task, feeling much more

relieved, she started to head back. She walked, and walked, and walked.

What the hell?

She had walked into the woods in a straight line. She was certain of it. Now she was following the same trek out of the woods, but the edge of the woods was nowhere to be found.

"Hello?! Bennett? Jordan?!" she tried to yell, but she was still too hoarse.

Hearing nothing, she made a mad dash for what she assumed to be the direction of the road. But it seemed that no matter how far she ran, the woods continued to stretch for miles and miles, all around her.

She looked about, surveying the landscape; looking for something, *anything* that looked familiar.

Wait. What—? Something did catch her eye. It hadn't been there before, had it? It couldn't have. The forest had been so dark, surely she'd have seen it if so. But there, only a few yards away from her, the sun's rays came flooding down on a spot where there were no trees. Walking closer, Andie realized that the light stretched for some distance, in a straight line. Wait a minute. *This is a road!* Andie gasped. She hadn't noticed before, and without the sunlight coming in, she would've never spotted it, for it was buried under a century of dead pine needles and rotting foliage. Surely this road had to lead out of the forest. Once again, Andie bolted as fast as she could, up the road.

After about a half a mile, she stopped dead in her tracks. The road hadn't led her back to her car, instead Andie found herself in a massive clearing near the edge of the cliff.

Oh.

My.

God.

Andie couldn't think of anything else to say. A million thoughts were racing through her mind. This was it. She'd finally found it. The very thing that had brought her to Maine was now staring her in the face.

The charred remains of a grand mansion stood between Andie and the endless sea which lay roaring behind it. It was just like the picture. The glass-less windows peered down at her, like a predator looking upon its prey. The roof had long since collapsed, and the stone walls were slathered in ash, but the ruins still stood proud and majestic, perching upon a lush green carpet of soft grass.

Time to start the next chapter of this book.

Her emotions teetered between frantic nerves and

boundless excitement. She made her way up the sweeping stone steps, stopping at the front entrance. A heavy pair of splintering wooden doors still stood, devotedly holding their charge to keep out the outside world. She could hear her heartbeat pounding in her ears, as she reached out for the rusty iron handles. Though they looked surprisingly capable, the doors opened for her with no effort. A blast of stale, damp air came rushing out of the open doors.

From the porch, Andie could see that the front room was a great hall. Though the walls were marked with the fire's destruction, the traces of grandeur were still ever-present. At the far end of the hall, a sweeping marble staircase prominently rose to the second floor. Andie shrieked with excitement. She had dreamed of this day, of this very moment, and still, standing here, this was even more perfect than she could have ever hoped for.

Alright, Andie. Let's do this.

She drew in a deep breath, then drew one foot over the threshold.

Honk, honk!

She stopped at the sound of her car's horn.

Shit! Not now, she thought.

Andie had just convinced herself to pretend she hadn't

heard the horn, and venture on, when,

honk, honk, HOOONNNKKK!!!

"Alright, alright!"

There was no use in trying to explore while she had someone breathing down her neck. She wanted to be able to take her time and savor every moment.

Andie pulled the doors shut, descended the stone steps, and began the long journey up the road; certain her car must be at the other end. It was.

"I was worried I was gonna have to send Jordan in after ya," Bennett said with a laugh.

Andie's car was now sitting back on the road, on all fours.

"She's good as new, or she will be after a good car wash," he laughed again.

A car wash, *indeed*. The car was caked in mud, but seemed to be fine otherwise.

"Thank you both, so much," she said.

"Think nothin' of it."

"Bennett, how long have you lived in Hollingshead?" she asked casually.

"My whole life. Born and raised. Why?"

"So you know the history of—"

"Urban legends," he cut her off. "Ghost stories, nothin' more," he continued.

"Even so, I find them fascinating. I know Julia doesn't want to talk about it…but I can tell that you do. Do you know anything about the disappearances that happened up here?"

Bennett's face fell.

"A few people came up here to commit suicide. *That's all*. Not really the sort of thing someone like you outta be worryin' about. It'd keep you up at night."

Clearly, Julia's threat had gotten to him too. He wasn't going to give her anything she could use.

"Enough talk about such things," Bennett said. "We've gotta get you back to town. Julia called and said your friend came by the house, lookin' for ya."

"My friend?" Andie asked.

CHAPTER 9

Max had already started drinking before Andie walked into the bar. He had, in fact, gotten a two-hour head start, so he was feeling more than a little buzzed. He sat there, staring hard into his highball of Scotch, feeling very, very sorry for himself. The dark, smokey atmosphere of this dive only added to the unhappiness that its patrons carried in with them. Every unfortunate soul that wandered in, in search of release, certainly wasn't going to find it here.

Andie spotted Max immediately. Her mind instantly went back to the night of his dad's funeral. Even from across the room, with his back to her just like before, shoulders hunched over just like before, head hung low just like…well you get it. The irony wasn't lost on Andie. Here she was, once again, standing in the doorway of a bar. Sure, it wasn't some posh joint in SoHo, like last time, it was just some cheap, hole-in-the-wall, watering hole. But by the look of Max, it was serving its purpose. He was clearly drunk. But that's where the similarities stopped. No matter what was said tonight, no matter how distraught, no matter how much she wanted to make things right with him, there'd be no hooking-up tonight. That's for damn sure. She hadn't kept her promise to call him the last time they'd spoken and that meant she'd have to do some damage control; and more than that, she decided that now was the time to tell Max where they stood.

"Sorry, Max."

Her tone was apologetic, but not at all weak. She made sure to sound firm in order to keep herself on task. In order to keep herself from falling for him all over again.

Max whirled around to face her. His heavy eyes tried to focus on her. His expression completely aloof.

"Sorry?"

Max laughed sarcastically.

"For what? Oh! That's right. I'll call you, Max."

Another sarcastic laugh. Then he pulled out his phone and began scrolling through the call history.

"Wait a minute," he continued. "What the hell? This

can't be right."

"Max, let me explain…"

"Shhh."

He threw up a finger, still looking down at his phone. Then went on.

"That's odd. I can't see where you called me back. But, I mean, surely you did. You *must have*. You said you *would…*"

"Max, if you'd let me explain—"

"No! No, you don't get to talk. I get to talk. You never call. *Never*. It's always me calling you. Dammit, for the life of me, I can't figure you out, Andie. What's more, I can't figure out why in the hell that…that I'm in love with you."

His eyes, red and puffy, erupting up with tears. They rose to meet Andie's.

"I love you, Andie," he said, pitifully.

Andie's chest fell hard, like the wind had been knocked out of her. This was it, no time to be chicken-shit about it anymore. Max deserved the truth. She felt as though it was the least she could do.

Cut this boy loose, Andie. But let him down gently.

"Max, you have no idea how much I care for you. Really."

She tenderly took his hand in hers. Then continued.

"And please believe me when I say that I love you too."

Max knew there was a *but* coming somewhere in here.

"But, I love you like a brother. The brother I've always wanted, but never had. I found that in you."

Max threw his head back and rolled his eyes.

"Unbelievable. Un-*fuckin'* believable. Is this supposed to make me feel better? *Huh?* Or are you just trying to make me feel like shit? 'Cause you're doing a damn fine job of that."

"It's true. God as my witness, it's true."

She held her hand up, piously.

"Max, do you know what a *man-eater* is?"

He threw a heavy fist down on the bar.

"C'mon, Andie! That's bullshit, and you know it! If you don't want anything to do with me, just fuckin' say so, OK? I'm a big boy, alright? I can take it!"

He was making a scene now. Both he and Andie scanned the dark room, realizing all eyes were on them.

"Why don't you all mind your own goddamn business, huh?!" Max shouted into the dark, haziness of the bar.

"Is everything alright over here?" inquired the bartender, playing the role of a teacher on lunchroom duty.

"We're fine, thank you," Andie said politely, then turned back to Max.

"Max, listen to me."

He just stared off, ignoring her.

"Max!" she snapped.

She grabbed his face and turned it to face hers.

"I know you can take it, that's why I'm telling you this."

She gained her composure, then went on.

"I know this sounds like bullshit. If I were you, I wouldn't believe it either, but I promise you that it's true. All of it," she took a deep breath, then let it out. "I can count on one hand the number of people that I've shared this with. But, like I said, I care about you, I know I can trust you. Anytime I allow myself to get into a committed relationship, every time that I get close to a guy, I start looking for reasons to bail. It's not just self-sabotage, it's like I steal their soul or something. I don't just discard them, I ruin them. It doesn't just end; it blows up and leaves them scarred for life. I wish I could explain why, but I honestly don't know. The best I can figure, it goes back to my childhood. Everything I told you about my parents, about my life growing up, was a lie, Max. Truth is, I hate my parents. I left home at sixteen and haven't spoken to them since. From my earliest memories, I can remember having these nightmares. Horrible nightmares. Dreams that left me paralyzed with fear. When I told my parents about them, they told me I would outgrow them. As I got older, they stopped believing me altogether. They thought that I was just acting out, for attention. And then, one day, they'd had enough. They did something—" she closed her eyes to reflect on that distant moment. A moment that she was now reliving. "I thought we were going to *Disney World*, can you believe it?"

For the first time, Andie felt herself start to cry about it. Hesitantly, she went on,

"They dropped me off on the front steps, handed me my bags, then drove away. I kept watching the car as it faded into the horizon. I told myself that it was some cruel, practical joke; that they'd turn the car around, pick me up, and we'd laugh about it all the way to *Disney World*. But they didn't come back."

Her voice was trembling now. Max looked tenderly at her, and gently wiped a tear from her eye. She smiled at him, then continued.

"I suppose something good did become of my time spent there, though. There was this one doctor, Doctor Remi, and he believed me. It was the first time I'd ever had someone look me in the eye and say that I wasn't crazy. That felt…so good. He taught me how to control my dreams. A year. My parents left me in that hospital for a fuckin' year. Probably trying to decide whether they still wanted this crazy, basket-case for a daughter," she laughed to lighten the moment, then became serious once more.

"Finally they came to take me home. But, to this day, I've never forgiven them."

"And what about your dreams?" he asked.

"Since I knew how to control them, they no longer scared me. I knew I could always find a way out. Eventually, they just…went away…but I never forgot them. I kept journals, and I wrote down every single one. Eventually, I wrote them into stories. You've even published some of them," she smiled at him. "In my own, weird sort of way, it was very cathartic. You see, I figured if I wrote them into stories, they became fiction, and were no longer a part of my reality."

"Wow," Max said. "That's a lot. I mean…I can't imagine. That's more than anyone should ever have to go through. Especially a child. Andie, I'm so sorry."

"So, every time I feel myself getting too close to someone, every time I allow myself to start feeling vulnerable, I just remember the sight of my parents driving away, and never once looking back. I freeze up. And then, I bail. I abandon them before they have the chance to abandon me. Max, I don't want to do that to you. I won't."

"Andie look at me."

She kept looking down. Max gently took her by the chin, then turned her face towards his.

"I promise you this," he continued. "I will never, *ever*, abandon you. No matter what, I would die before I let you down."

Andie gave a weak smile.

"Don't make promises you can't keep."

"I never do," he smiled back.

He truly meant this. Max knew what he had to say in this moment, what he had to do…that didn't mean he wanted to. In fact, this was just about the last thing he'd planned on saying to Andie tonight.

"…and" he continued, "…if you say you need space, I'll give you space. From now on, I'll work on keeping my distance. But just know, if you ever need anything, or if you ever change your mind, just know that I'll always be right here, waiting. No matter what, I've got you."

Max quickly looked back down at his Scotch, to keep from crying.

Andie smiled, wider than she had in years.

"You're one of the good ones, you know that?" she said, kissing Max on the cheek.

Max didn't look up, but Andie could see him smiling too.

She could think of a million things to say, to keep the conversation going, but she stopped herself. They were in a good place right now. They were where they needed to be. Best to leave things as they were, after all, some part of her might convince herself to go after round two with Max; especially if she stayed for a drink.

"Well, it's getting late. I'm gonna call it a night," Andie grabbed her coat and stood up. Just then a loud crash of thunder shook the building, rattling the windows.

"Sounds like another storm is moving in..." Max began.

"Nothing I can't handle. I already weathered one, remember?" she said laughing.

"At least let me make sure you get back to your—"

"Space. Remember?" she politely cut him off. "This is your chance to make good on your promise."

Max nodded and sat back down.

"I'll call you when I get back to New York," she said, "and yes, I *promise* this time."

And with that, Andie was gone.

Max's mind was still a fury of emotions. His thoughts rumbled like the storm outside. At least he'd finally told Andie how he felt. At least he finally knew how she felt about him.

Even if that meant there was no chance for a *them*.

"Tough break, huh buddy?"

Max looked up to see the bartender pretending to wipe up a spill on the bar next to him.

"I mean, a hot little number like that—"

In an instant, Max grabbed him by the shirt and was so close that their faces were practically touching.

"That's the woman I *love*, you sonofabitch! Don't talk about her as if she were just some *piece of ass*!"

The bartender pushed himself away and threw up his hands in surrender.

"Whoa, whoa! Easy man. I don't want any *trouble*."

CHAPTER 10

It was already raining by the time Andie climbed in her car. She shook out her hair and started the car, turning on the heat in an effort to relax.

Part of her couldn't believe she told Max.

The other part of her felt so relieved that she did.

Now she wouldn't have to tap-dance around him, trying to ignore his all-but subtle hints. Him staring at her when he thought she wasn't looking. Now they could just work on being friends, like they used to. That's what she wanted. At least, that's what she told herself.

The rain was coming down in sheets now, almost like last night's episode. Andie knew that she should go back to the *Airbnb. It's storming too hard. I don't wanna get stuck up there again.* She was trying to convince herself, but she knew it was useless. That house was waiting for her. It was calling for her. *That's stupid, Andie. Houses can't talk to you.* Except, this one, it did. It called her, almost by name; and, finally, she was ready to respond to it. She rolled her neck, flailed her fingers around the grip of the steering wheel, and took a few deep breaths. Then she put the car into drive, pulled out of her parking space, and left the parking lot.

With such poor visibility, Andie could barely see the road in front of her, so it's not unexpected that she didn't see the pickup truck that had pulled out behind her. From a safe distance, it followed, watching, mimicking her every move. When she turned, it turned. When she sped up or slowed down, so did it; all the way through town, then up the long, steep coastal road.

When Andie spotted the giant rock at the bend in her path, she knew the road to the house lay just beyond it. She carefully pulled up to the edge of the forest, spotted the overgrown driveway, then slowly turned down it. The mysterious truck that had been following her, stopped at the edge of the woods, but didn't drive into them like she had. Instead, it parked itself inconspicuously behind the rock. The driver turned off the lights, killed the engine, then both the driver and passenger doors opened, and two men got out of the truck, and they ventured into the woods on-foot.

Andie's car emerged into the clearing at the far end of the hidden road. There was the house, still waiting for her. She could almost feel its anticipation. She parked her car and ventured out into the pouring rain. The black sky pulsed with lightning; which was as beautiful as it was terrifying. The rain had brought a thick blanket of fog with it, which encased the house like a ghostly shroud. Armed with the emergency flashlight from her roadside kit, she once again climbed the stairs and pushed open the doors to the mansion.

The sound of rain, filtering in through the collapsed ceiling, echoed through the massive room which lay just before her. As she listened, she felt like her ears were playing tricks on her, for now, instead of the tapping of the water, it sounded more like faint whispers.

C'mon Andie, you're freaking yourself out. You've driven all the way up here. You've waited for this. You're ready for this. It's time.

No sooner had she shaken those thoughts from her mind, the sound of whispers grew closer, grew louder.

Get a hold of yourself. No time to wuss out now. Let's go.

First one foot, then the other, and now she was standing *inside* the house.

Turning on the flashlight, Andie scanned the room. As her nerves allowed, she moved further and further into the house. Before she knew it, she'd walked all the way across the massive room stopping at the foot of the grand staircase. She marveled at the beauty of the exquisite marble stairs, and the ornately carved railing that beckoned her upstairs. With a finger, she wrote her name in the soot which covered the surface. From the black contrast of the sediment, the gleaming white marble was now brought back to life where a cursive script read, *Andie.*

"Andie," came a whisper from behind her.

She whipped around, shining the flashlight.

"Who's there?!"

"Andie," the whisper came from the other side this time.

Her heartbeat was racing, and her whole body was shaking. This time, it wasn't a dream. She was awake. She pinched herself to be sure. *Ouch!* Yep. Wide awake.

"I'm not afraid of you!" she shouted arbitrarily, unsure of where she should direct her yelling. "But maybe you're afraid of me, *huh*? If you're not afraid of me, why don't you show yourself?"

"I'm just playing a game, Andie. I *love* playing games," the whisper laughed.

"Well I don't want to play games! If you don't wanna show yourself, then I'm leaving," she said, turning to leave.

"I know why you're here, Andie. You want to know things. I'll tell you Andie, I'll tell you everything. But I need something from you, in return."

"What do you want?" Andie asked, soberly.

"I'm up here, Andie. Come up here, and all will be revealed to you," the voice called from upstairs.

Something in Andie knew she shouldn't. Talking to strange, disembodied voices was one thing, but following them upstairs in what must be, for all intents and purposes, a creepy haunted house…that was just crazy. *But then again,* Andie reassured herself, *I like a little crazy.*

Grabbing onto the railing, Andie slowly climbed the stairs. Her flashlight did little to illuminate the darkness, this house seemed to steal the light.

"That's it, Andie. You're almost there. Just a few more steps."

The whispers were growing closer now, growing stronger. Andie stopped at the top of the stairs.

"OK, I'm here. Now it's your turn."

A dark shadow, like billowing smoke, swept across the floor, at her feet. Then slowly rose. As the smoke took the form of a man, Andie suddenly realized that she'd seen it before; she was both calmed and confused by this fact.

"It's you," she said.

CHAPTER 11

K*nock, knock, knock. What the hell?* Max slowly worked to push his eyelids apart. *Wow, that hurts.* Sunlight filled his hotel room. Rolling over on his back, Max looked down and tried to count his toes. There were definitely more than ten. *Dammit, I'm still drunk.* The knocking came again. Some bastard stood on the other side of the door to Max's room, intent on pounding as loud as humanly possible.

"Who's there?" Max managed to call out.

No reply, just more knocking.

"Goddamn it, do you know what time it is? It's…" Max lurched forward to read the big, red numbers on the nightstand's LED alarm clock. "It's seven o'clock!" he continued.

Max rolled out of bed and collapsed into a miserable heap on the floor. *Dammit, c'mon legs, work with me here.* He clumsily rose to his feet and stumbled toward the door. Another knock.

"Alright, alright! Geez, keep your pants on, will ya?" he said, at the very same moment he realized that he wasn't wearing any.

A quick check of the peephole revealed the masochistic bastard, who delighted in waking people up at seven o'clock in the morning. It was a young police officer.

Shit! What did I do?

Max thought about last night. He'd drank, a lot, but he still remembered everything that had happened. He and Andie talked, she left, he stayed at the bar until it closed at one A.M. He was far too drunk to drive, but sober enough to know that he shouldn't, so he walked back to the hotel. He could remember that much, so why would an officer be here, knocking on his door?

"Mister Tate? I know you're in there," came a voice from the other side of the door.

Max slapped his face a few times, in a desperate attempt to sober up. He tried to fasten the chain before opening the door but gave up when he saw at least three of them. He cleared his throat and opened the door.

"Good morning officer, how can I help you, officer?"

Shit, I said officer twice.

Though it wouldn't have mattered.

Max was *clearly* drunk.

His sentence came slurring out as if it were one continuous word. Not only that, but he smelt like a human Molotov cocktail. Max forced an awkward smile, as if this were any ordinary morning conversation.

"Mister Tate I'm gonna need you to come with me, please."

"On what charges?" Max insisted.

"Just put on your pants, and come with me please, sir."

The officer was nothing but business. Whatever answers Max wanted, he wasn't gonna get them from this asshole.

Max threw on a pair of pants, grabbed a handful of water to splash his face, another to slick back his hair, and poured half a container of T*ic Tacs* down his throat, but now felt like he should have taken the whole thing.

The officer didn't put Max in handcuffs, and he'd even let Max ride up front with him in the squad car. If he was under arrest, it certainly didn't seem like it.

When they arrived at the station, the officer led Max into a waiting room, gestured to him to have a seat, and left. The station, while in good repair, looked like it hadn't been updated since it was built in, *probably*, the nineteen-fifties. Pistachio green walls rose ten or twelve feet high; anchored to a faded, pinewood floor. Schoolhouse pendant lights hung, nostalgically, from the curved plaster ceiling overhead.

Max sat alone, in a row of old, heavy, wooden chairs. The only other soul in the room was a sixty-something secretary, who sat pecking away at an old, manual typewriter. She didn't look up when Max and the officer entered the room, she just sat there, tap, tap, tapping away. Max quickly found himself annoyed by the dissonance caused by the tempo of her typing, against the ticking of the old analog clock which hung high on the wall.

As his hangover was now in full swing, he cursed the secretary and her stupid typing.

Ugh, shut up, Hazel!

He assumed her name was Hazel, because, well it would be rather fitting with the aged décor of this room, wouldn't it? That, and, well, she looked like a Hazel.

"Welcome to Mayberry," he moaned under his breath.

The secretary looked up for the first time, rolled her eyes, and fell right back into her typing.

Just then, a door flew open across the room. A uniformed officer emerged from a corner office. He was older, stockier, and based on his patchwork, higher ranking than the one who'd brought Max here.

"Mister Tate," he said in an annoyed tone.

Max looked up.

The officer gave a *come here* motion with his finger, before turning and disappearing back into the office.

"Hazel, it's been a pleasure," Max said, standing up.

She gave him a confused look as he walked away.

"Mister Tate, please, have a seat," said the officer.

His mustache inched back and forth like a caterpillar on his upper lip and his fat cheeks flapped as he spoke. Max stared at him, then he looked at the other man in the room. Like the officer, he was also middle-aged, but slender. He was dressed in a brown tweed suit, with elbow patches, and a boring brown tie. A brass name plate on the desk read *Tilman Bond-Mayor.*

"Am I under arrest?" Max asked.

"Not technically, no," said the officer.

"In that case, I think I'll stand. I don't expect I'll be

staying very long."

"Mister Tate," Tilman began, "Sheriff Walker and I have been monitoring your behavior around town, and I must say, we don't like what we've seen."

"I haven't even been here twenty-four hours."

"Well, *no*, but your accomplice has been here for about a week now."

"My accomplice?"

"You know damn well I'm talking about Andie Sterling," said the mayor, impatiently.

"The two of you were spotted together at Donovan's Bar last night," added the sheriff.

"My wife reads that incessant garbage that Miss Sterling churns out, the stuff that you shamelessly print. Once the good folks of this town figured out who Miss Sterling was, any idiot with *Google* could've figured out who you were," the mayor continued.

"Alright fellas, ya got me," Max turned to Tilman, and went on. "I do know Andie; I *do* print the stories she writes. But I'm not some tabloid editor. I work in book publishing; big difference. And last time I checked, visiting a small, New England town wasn't exactly illegal; in fact, I thought tourism was supposed to be *good* for your economy."

"Well of course it is, mister—"

"Then what crimes have we committed?"

"None, per se, but—"

"Then what the *hell* am I doing here?" Max demanded.

Mayor Bond almost snapped back, but collected himself, then calmly continued.

"Of course we love tourism. That's not the problem here. The problem is Miss Sterling's behavior."

"What are you talking about?"

"She's asking questions," said the sheriff, "and we don't like it."

Max threw back his head and laughed, making light of the accusation.

"Welcome to Mayberry!"

"Is this a joke to you?" implored Sheriff Walker, sternly.

"Oh no! Of course not," Max laughed, "I mean *this*, this is serious…what do you think would be an appropriate punishment? Personally, I'd vote the electric chair."

"Mister Tate, as you're well aware, Hollingshead has a bit of a checkered past," said Tilman.

Max sarcastically faked a look of concern.

THE HAND THAT FEEDS YOU

"Oh really? Hmm, no I wasn't aware—"

"The very sort of salacious gossip that you like to write about."

"*Again*, not my line of work."

"As you can imagine, these are the sort of things that can damage the reputation of a small town like ours. And we've tried very hard to keep such matters sealed."

"So, you censor history?" Max asked.

"Just the ghost stories. The dreadful, ugly things that don't do no good for anybody," the sheriff chimed in.

"It's not your job to decide what people *should* and *shouldn't* be allowed to know," Max narrowed his gaze at both men.

"And it's not *your job* to dig up dirt on a town in which you have *no business*," Tilman said. "In fact, the *only* story of yours that I'd like to read, is the one that says Maxwell Tate, a third-rate editor from New York City, enjoyed an uneventful evening in Hollingshead Maine, before returning home to New York, where he *belonged*. And the good folks of town never heard from him, *ever* again."

"Nothing would please me more than to get the hell outta this shitty little town. As luck would have it, I'm returning home today," Max practically cheered.

"I think that would be wise," said the mayor.

"And, maybe you're right, maybe there isn't anything to those old ghost stories after all," Max continued.

"Of course not," Tilman agreed.

"But ya know," Max said with a smile, "I think there just might be a story here. One involving elected officials, using their political position as a means to intimidate those who haven't broken any laws, *your words* not *mine*, in hopes of suppressing public information."

The eyes of both men grew wide with this, but they said nothing.

"Actually," Max continued, "maybe we should just throw both stories at the wall and see which one sticks, huh?"

Max laughed, then turned to leave.

The silence of the room was deafening.

When he reached the door, Max stopped and turned back around for one last word.

"Oh, by the way, gentleman, I did find something that I think you'll both find very useful."

Max shoved both hands into his pockets.

The mayor cleared his throat, then tentatively asked,

"And, what is that, Mr. Tate?"

Max pulled out both hands, each holding up the

middle finger.

"These, I got one for each of ya."

CHAPTER 12

That first week back in New York was a cold one. In every sense of the word. In the final weeks leading up to his excursion, the dog days of summer had been holding on for dear life—wrapping the city in a dense, muggy sweater; trapping everything and everyone in an uncomfortable sea of humidity. But now, Fall had taken over, and with it those cool days and chilly nights had brought some level of reprieve.

Autumn colors had painted the lush groves of trees in Central Park. The streets were burning in warm hues of crimson, amber, and goldenrod. Though burning leaves in the city was not allowed, the faint whiff of them would occasionally be carried in on the winds from the more rural townships that encircled upper Manhattan, or sometimes from just across the Hudson.

So why did he still feel so depressed? Max lived for this. Fall was his favorite season; by a long-shot. The clothes. The chilly nights. The cozy fires. All of it. But no amount of pumpkin spice lattes could drown the void he felt ever since he'd come back from Maine.

He promised himself it was over. Andie was just a friend. Less than that, if he had to be honest. She worked for him. He was her boss, and it was inappropriate. So why did he still feel like he wasn't over her? He just needed to find a distraction. Soon enough things would be back to normal, he just needed to get through the next week or so. Yeah, that's all he needed to do. Just wait it out.

To begin, he buried himself in his work. He'd been out of the office for about two weeks, and because of his absence there were a ton of fires left to put out. *This place would go to shit without me.* Max cursed his junior editors for their incompetence, for their inability to handle even the most menial of tasks without his direction. Yet, he secretly loved the respect it earned him, that and the job security.

In his free time, he went to a couple *Mets* games; then remembered why he wasn't a *Mets* fan. *Is anyone really a Mets fan?* He played a few rounds of racquetball with Kyle from accounting. Generally, this was his go-to stress reliever, because Kyle was terrible at racquetball. But then Kyle began winning and not just by a little. Literally, Max was getting his ass handed to him by Kyle. *Stupid Kyle.* And the dick was getting cocky about it. That's when Max knew he needed to try something else.

One night, as he was leaving the health club, he decided to hop on the train. For anyone else this would be a perfectly normal thing; but not for Max. Max hated the train. His trust-fund upbringing had instilled in him the belief that only poor people took the train; though he'd never openly admit that he felt that way. Needless to say, he felt a little uncomfortable dodging the glances, either real or imagined, from his fellow train-riders. He wasn't from their world. He didn't belong here. They knew it and he knew it.

After about an hour, totally lost, unable to follow the train route posted above the subway doors, he decided to get off at the next stop and order a car service home; something he should've done when he left the racquetball court.

Max had barely reached the steps to the street level when he realized that he knew where he was; well, kinda. The neighborhood looked familiar. He'd been there before. The night was chilly, but perfectly so. He walked three blocks

East, as if by instinct. Then he looked up. That was the building alright. That was her apartment, fourth floor, second set of windows from the right; the ones with the fire escape. But the apartment was dark. Andie wasn't home.

It had been a week or so since he'd let Andie walk out of that smokey, old bar in Maine. If he was being honest, he knew that it had been exactly nine days. He'd told himself that it was over. Told himself that he'd already moved on. There were bigger things out there waiting for him. Andie meant nothing to him; but it was all bullshit, and he knew it. He was miserable. Still head over heels for the girl that he'd promised to give space. Space and time. He'd given her nine days after all, how much time did she need?

He wondered where she was tonight. Who was she out with? Some other guy? Someone to help her forget Max? To make him jealous? He felt creepy and obsessive for tying to figure it all out. He felt stupid because there really was no way of knowing. Had she even come back to the city, yet? Surely she had. She originally planned to stay a week. But she said she'd call when she got back to town. Yeah, he'd heard that line before.

OK, Max. You've seriously gotta stop this. You said you'd give her time. You said you could be a friend.

But a friend would worry about her, *right*? What if she never made it back? What if she was stranded? What if she was in trouble? That idiot mayor and sheriff didn't seem like the type that would concern themselves with helping her out, if she needed them.

He looked at his reflection in the store-front window, then read the neon sign next to the glowing hand before him. *Palm Readings by Madam Luna*. Max groaned, *at least she might know if Andie's come home, yet.*

He cautiously opened the door, and stepped inside. A small bell tingled, welcoming him. The shop was dim, and bedecked with flickering candles in every corner. A gilded Buddha smiled to greet him while a blue-skinned Kali statue judged him, disapprovingly. Obviously she knew he didn't belong here, either. Paintings of nude women were plastered across the walls while colorful scarves spun from cheap fabrics filled in the barren gaps. There were large floor pillows scattered about for lounging, and, of course, two chairs flanking a round table in the center of the room, draped with long tablecloth and showcasing, *what else*, a crystal ball. There was a small counter in the corner, with a cash register, for selling incense, tarot card packs, and other cheap junk. Behind the counter, a pair of heavy, red velvet curtains were drawn back by gilded ropes.

Aside from all of this kitsch, the store was empty. Where was the store's proprietor? The so-called psychic, Madam Luna?

"Hello?" he called out.

In the back room, behind the velvet curtains, he heard someone knock something over, and a crash of small, breakable items clattered onto the floor.

"Shit!" a voice whispered in response. "Uh, just a moment!"

Guess she didn't see me coming, typical. Max joked to himself. By this point, he almost felt embarrassed for whomever Madam Luna was, and had half-convinced himself to just leave. Spare her the guilt of showing her face after she'd just broken, what he assumed to be her favorite tea set. He played the moment in his mind, and cringed. He was just turning to leave, when a woman emerged from between the curtains; poised, like the lead actress taking her triumphant bow, at the curtain call of a Broadway show.

The woman was busy to look-at. If that makes sense. Visually-loud, somewhat stout, with pale skin and jet-black hair, which was obviously dyed, and cut into a short bob. *Or maybe it was a wig?* She had to be in her mid-forties to early-fifties. She was nothing if not a caricature of what one must assume to be the very stereotype of a cheap psychic. Gold crescent moon earrings dangled from her earlobes, weak from age and years of carrying more than their fair share of gaudy jewelry.

"There you are! I've been waiting for you..." the voice was masked in a forced, gypsy accent.

Oh here we go, thought Max.

"Uh huh. I'm sure. Listen, I just came in to—"

"Stop!" the woman interrupted. "Madam Luna knows why you've come."

"Is that a fact? OK, then. Tell me."

She closed her eyes, drew her fingertips together, then placed them to her brow; deep in thought.

"You've come in search of something."

"Amazing," he feigned in underwhelming sarcasm.

She continued.

"You seek advice...about...your career."

"Exactly!"

He was playing her, in an attempt to prove she was a fraud. Sure, he was being mean, but he had his reasons. For one, Max was a realist. A very factual, analytical person; sometimes to a fault. But he also hated that there were those who would willingly take advantage of someone, for their own personal gain.

Psychics. Charlatans, all of them, he silently thought to himself. So, he decided, he wasn't being a bully, he was just giving her a taste of her own medicine.

"What else?" he went on, sounding genuine this time.

"You have an opportunity for a promotion…"

"Yes! And?"

"You are worried that accepting this new position would be a mistake?"

"Oh my god! You are amazing!"

"Thank you, I know."

"So? Should I take it? *Please* Madam Luna, I have to know. You're my only hope," he almost burst out laughing at his own, desperate performance.

She opened her eyes, looked at him, and smiled.

"The fates want to tell me, but they need a little encouragement."

Then she stuck out a hand, signaling that he'd need to pay her before she told him any more. That's it, he'd had his fun.

Time to call her bluff.

This time, he did laugh.

He cackled.

He let it all out.

Madam Luna stood there, confused.

"What is so funny?"

The gypsy accent was gone now, replaced with that of a native New Yorker.

"I'm sorry, I'm sorry. I just have to ask...do you actually believe the shit you spew? Because, I mean you do seem pretty convincing."

Her face fell.

"Get out."

"Have you ever thought about taking your show on the road? Because, I think you could make a killing."

He was being a little too mean now, and he knew it. He just couldn't stop.

"Let's see how well you can improv. *Tell me, Madam Luna, was I a dog in a past life? Because I really feel like I was.*"

"I said get the hell out of my store!"

She shot a swift hand out, pointing to the door.

Then Max remembered, he really had gone in to ask for her help. Probably too late for that now. *Sonofabitch. There I go with my fucking mouth again.* This lady, phony bologna or not, she likely saw the coming and goings of everyone living the apartments above her. If anyone knew about Andie's whereabouts, whether she had come back to the city or not, this lady knew.

"Look," he began, apologetically, "I am sorry, I was just having a little fun. I didn't mean to let it go that far."

He threw up his hands in apologetic surrender.

"Why are you still in my store? Don't you know when you're not wanted?"

Damn. After the last week, that one hit a little too close to home.

"Funny thing is, I do know, but sometimes I have a hard time moving on…"

"No shit," she said, annoyed.

"The truth is, I did come in here to ask for your help."

"Are you fucking kidding me? You come into *my* store, mock me, insult me, and now you have the audacity to ask for *my* help? You know I think you just might've been a dog in a former life, because you've come back as a worthless piece of shit now."

He held up a twenty.

"Does this help my chances?" he asked, flashing that famous smile.

It seemed to work. He could see her softening up. She took the bill, and stashed it beneath her shirt.

"It's a start."

Her countenance returned to an all-business state.

"Now," she went on, "what is it I can do for you?"

"I'm looking for someone."

"I thought you didn't believe in my powers," she said, skeptically.

"She lives here, in this building. Fourth floor. Late twenties. Auburn hair?"

"Oh, so you're looking for Andie," she said in a disapproving tone; one that gave Max pause.

"Uh, yeah, you know her?"

"Then you must be Max," even more accusatory this time.

"She's told you about me," Max realized aloud.

The woman retrieved the twenty dollars from her bra and went to hand it back to him.

"Listen Mr. Tate. I'm afraid I can't help you."

He looked at the money, but didn't take it back.

"Um, why not?"

"Listen to me, take your money, leave my shop, and move on with your life. This is sage advice; free of charge…

something I never offer."

He took offense at this.

"What do you mean? You don't even know me!"

"I know that you love Andie. And she has feelings for you. But the two of you are on different paths. You aren't destined to be together. This wasn't decided by me, it's in your cards. Like I told Andie—" she stopped herself before finishing the thought.

"What?!" he demanded.

"Nothing, forget I said it. Here, take your money and go."

"Unbelievable. Un-fucking-believable!"

"Mr. Tate, please…"

"Zip it, Miss Cleo! Look, you don't get to tell me what to do. You don't get to tell anyone what to do! I mean, what right do you have to tell Andie that she shouldn't be in love with me, huh?"

"I know you don't believe in my powers, and that's fine. I don't have to explain myself to you. But I do care about Andie. I've seen what will happen if the two of you wind up together. Trust me, it wouldn't lead to happiness. It would only lead to destruction."

"The choice isn't yours to make! Even if this whole,

fucking thing blows up in my face, I wanna see it through, because I wanna know for myself whether or not it's meant to be; and Andie should have that right, *too*. And you say you care about Andie, well so do I! I love her more than I've ever loved anyone in my life! In fact that's why I came into this place to ask for your help. She was supposed to be back by now, but it doesn't look like she is; and it's got me worried. If you truly cared about her you'd help me by giving me some real answers, not any of this bogus shit you sell to the people that waltz into your store and shove a few bucks in your face."

She just stood there, contemplating the truth of what he'd said. He was right. It *wasn't* her decision. It was their lives, and sometimes people have to make their own mistakes in order to move on. More than just that, she was worried too, about Andie.

"You're right, Mr. Tate."

"I am? I mean, yes, of course I am."

"I meddle. I do. Especially when it's someone I care about. Andie is very special to me. She comes down to visit me nearly every day. Truth is, I've been worried about her too. She was supposed to be back days ago, but she hasn't even called. I've been feeding her cat, Thoreau. She loves that little guy. She wouldn't just leave him. She wouldn't just not come back. That's not like her. Something's not right, I can feel it. I can sense it."

Max sighed heavily.

"I feel it too."

He thought for a moment, then,

"I'm going back to Maine."

Without a word, Madam Luna began blowing out the candles.

"What are you doing?" Max asked.

"I'm coming with you," the psychic said, peeling the black wig off; revealing her true-ish, blonde hair.

"What, why?"

"You need my help," she said, wadding the cheap wig into her knock-off, Chinatown purse.

"Listen, Madam…"

"Luna."

"Right, I'm not trying to be a jerk, I really just think I'm better off alone—"

"Max, listen to me. You only know one side of Andie. There's another side of her that she's never shown you. Things she's never told you about herself. Trust me, you don't know her like I do. If you're going there to find her, then you're going to need my help."

Max knew she was right. The last time he had talked to Andie hadn't exactly gone over so well. Plus, if she was fine, how would he explain why he decided to come back to Maine? Madam...whatever her name was...provided that buffer. She said she felt worried, he could use her as an excuse.

"How do I look?" she asked, revealing her costume change; she was now just any typical, big-haired, Long Island...not-so-medium.

"Alright, fine," Max said. "I mean, *fine*, you can come with—"

"Good, we can discuss my fee on the way."

"Your *fee*?"

"And make sure to book us separate hotel rooms, now. I know your kind. I don't want no funny business!"

"Funny business? Ha! You honestly think that *I* would —"

"Hurry up and book the tickets, Max! Before they clear the upgrade list and all of the first class seats are full."

CHAPTER 13

"Ladies and gentlemen this is your captain speaking. Uh. We've got a few reports of moderate chop in the area. Could get a little bumpy here. Uh. We've got that seat belt sign on, so we do ask that you'd please take your seats and keep your seat belts securely fastened. Thank you."

Max didn't have to fasten his seat belt, it was already fastened; probably tighter than it needed to be. Afraid for a repeat of last time, he decided to skip the sleeping pill; but not the alcohol. Never the alcohol. Madam Luna looked down at his hands, holding the armrest in a death-grip.

"Nervous flyer, huh?"

"The spirits tell you that?" he laughed, sarcastically.

"They didn't have to, smart-ass."

She cued him to look at his posture. Leaning dramatically back into his seat, arms strapped down, you'd have to be an idiot not to notice how awkward he looked. He attempted to relax a bit.

"Sorry, that was a joke," he promised, "I'll stop."

She held up her drink.

"These are the only spirits I'm concerned with right now."

"I'll drink to that," Max said, clicking his glass with hers.

They both took a drink.

"That reminds me," she began, "why all this hatred? A skeptic is one thing, but you, you've got a score to settle with someone. I wanna know who."

"You first," he said, playfully. "You tell me your secrets and I'll tell you mine."

"What do you wanna know?" she took another sip of her drink.

"What made you wanna become a psychic? And Madam Luna? What kind of name is that anyway?"

"Well, let's see," she threw her head back and looked to the ceiling in reflective thought. "I suppose it all started when I was four or five. I lost both of my parents in a car accident."

"God. I'm sorry."

"It happens," she smiled. "But being a child, naturally I was left feeling rather lost and alone without them. I remembered watching a movie where someone held a séance to talk to a dead relative. Obviously I knew nothing about it, but I tried to recreate what I'd seen, or what I could remember from the movie…and you know what happened?"

"What?"

Max brought his seat upright.

"Nothing."

She laughed. Then continued.

"Well, not the first time. Or the second. Or even the third. But, eventually, one night, I felt something. I was trying to contact my parents, talking to them as if they were in the room with me, when I heard someone whispering in my ear. Telling me that they could hear me. Telling me that everything was going to be alright."

"And? What then?" Max asked.

"Well I screamed, obviously. I mean, Christ, it scared the shit out of me," she laughed. "But then, I calmed down. And I realized that I'd done something that I had been told couldn't be done. I had talked to my parents, or at least what I assumed to be my parents. And they'd talked back to me." She shook her head. "From that moment on, I knew that I was special. Not everyone could do this, but I could. I had been given this gift. And I wanted to use it to help people. To connect them to loved ones they'd lost. The more I worked at it, the more consistent I became. The more the voices would respond to me. They'd tell me things."

"What kinds of things?" Max asked, curiously.

"Sometimes it was good things, like how they missed their husband or wife. Or that they were proud of their children. And other times…"

She trailed off for a moment, lost in her thoughts, then she came back.

"And other times, it was sad things, dark things, things I didn't want to repeat. To tell the grieving widow. The one who'd come to me, lost and broken, asking for my help."

She looked gravely at Max.

"Sometimes, when they said those things, I worried that I wasn't talking to a lost loved one. But I was talking to something…else. Something…" she trailed off again, then returned with, "well, I suppose that's another discussion entirely."

Max sighed, heavily.

She laughed to lighten the mood.

"And as far as the name," she went on, "Madam Luna, well, let's just say that Sylvia Goldstein isn't exactly the sort of name that brings customers in the door. Besides, do you know how many of them there are in a Long Island phone book? Too—"

"Too goddamn many?" he interjected.

"Now who's the mind-reader, eh?" Sylvia laughed. "OK, hotshot, your turn. What's with all the hate? You seem like a nice guy. There's gotta be some reason."

This time Max threw *his* head back, reflectively. Carefully thinking about his words, composing himself so that he held it all together.

"A few months ago, my father passed away."

"Oh, Max, I'm sorry to hear that," said Sylvia.

"Thank you. It was…all very unexpected. Took us all by surprise; especially my mom. It's been the hardest on her. She, uh, she's had trouble accepting it. Trouble moving on, ya know?"

"Mmhmm."

"Because it all happened so fast, she's convinced that there was some kind of foul play. Something, we're missing. Something we didn't see."

"Well, that's understandable. When these things happen, suddenly, there's no closure. The grieved need their time to grieve. Sounds like she hasn't had that."

"Yeah, well…she's tried reaching out to him. Ever since he passed, she's been calling upon psychics to help her contact him. To give her the answers she's looking for."

"I see…"

"But, they aren't helping her. They're just taking her money, lots of money, to tell her the things she wants to hear. They're taking advantage of a poor woman, who's just trying to deal with losing the love of her life. And that…that…just doesn't sit well with me. You know? If they really wanted to help her they should just tell her to see a therapist. Someone to help her move on, ya know?"

He was on the verge of breaking down. His tenderness plucked at Sylvia's heartstrings; something she hadn't expected. He wasn't a total jerk, after all. He was hurting. Hurting just like his mother.

"Max, listen to me."

Sylvia took his hand, and looked him in the eye.

"When your mother talks to these people, how does she respond?"

"What do you mean?"

"Does she seem better? Or worse after talking to them?"

Max thought for a second.

"Better, I guess. But it's only because she's paying them to tell her what she wants to hear."

"Sounds to me like they're telling her what she needs to hear."

He took this in.

"I'm not saying you have to believe in what I do. I'm not saying that all mediums are good and honest. But your mother is grieving. She seeks closure. She needs that to be able to heal...to move on. When she seeks counsel with these people, she's getting just that. If it's making her feel better, then I think it's worth it to her, don't you?"

"I suppose so," he said, with glossy eyes.

"It's clear that you love your mother, and she's lucky to have someone like you."

Sylvia looked upward, then continued.

"And I know he's happy that you're still here, looking out for her." Her gaze fell back to him."You're a good son, Max."

"Thank you," his voice was barely above a whisper.

She smiled at him tenderly.

"Now, are you gonna let go of my hand, or do I need to get out the rape whistle?"

He almost burst out in laughter, releasing all the sad tension of the moment.

"I told you, I'm not that kind of psychic."

CHAPTER 14

It was just after noon. Even after they'd picked up the rental car, grabbed an early lunch, and drove from Bangor to Hollingshead, it was still too early to check-in to the hotel. So, they decided to head into town and start looking for clues. Better to hit the ground running, anyway. *Why waste any more time?* Max insisted.

"Holy moly. I thought you said this was a small town," Sylvia sat in the passenger seat, her eyes glued to the never-ending line of cars outside.

To say that the town was busy would be an understatement. Not a single parking space was left along any street and they were stuck in a traffic gridlock that made Max feel like he was back in Manhattan.

"Must be tourists. Everybody coming to New England

to see the Fall leaves," Max sighed.

He didn't really know where to start. He hadn't exactly planned this thing out. For starters, he knew where her *Airbnb* was. If she was still in town, that's likely where she was staying, so it made the most sense to begin there.

"Whoa. What's going on, here?" Sylvia pointed to a large crowd of people gathered in the courthouse square.

A large, white gazebo on the courthouse lawn acted as a stage, upon which the mayor, sheriff, and several city officials stood to address the crowd. It didn't seem like a joyful occasion. No one appeared to be happy. They just stood there, hanging on to every word of the mayor's speech.

Knowing it was pointless to try and find a parking spot, Max pulled the car off to the side of the street, turned off the engine, and unbuckled.

"Let's go check it out."

"...and, once again, the city would like to express its heartfelt gratitude to all of the volunteers, who've given their time on this search. I know I speak for, not only myself, but for the family of our beloved Tommy Irons, when I say, thank you. Together we will find Tommy, and bring him safely home."

The mayor was a true politician. A strong balance of

resolution and compassion in his delivery. But Max could read people; this man was worried. The crowd became a frenzy of outspoken questions and waving hands. An unbridled cacophony of voices, fighting to be the one heard, until one finally was.

"Mayor Bond, it's been seven days now. How long will the city continue its search?"

"We'll continue for as long as it takes. We will find him."

The mayor looked down at a man and woman in the front of the crowd. The two were crying and holding each other in consolation; Max assumed this must be Tommy's parents.

"Does the city have any leads?" came another voice.

"Are the disappearances starting again?" came yet another.

"What about our children?"

"Or our own safety?"

"Should we be afraid"

"Has it returned?!"

The crowd was out of control, now.

The mayor grabbed Sheriff Walker by the arm and threw him into center stage.

"Shut them down, now!" he growled through gritted teeth.

"Ladies and gentlemen! *Please!*" the sheriff shouted over them.

This did little to quiet the crowd. The questions continued.

"It's back!"

"And you're trying to cover it up, again!"

"We want answers!"

"Our lives are at stake!"

Walker tried harder.

"The Sheriff's Department is doing all we can to ensure the safety of our citizens!"

But no one listened, not even for a second. The crowd refused to be consoled.

Mayor Bond threw the sheriff back into the lineup of useless aldermen who stood upstage.

"If you want something done right…" he cursed under his breath; before turning to address the mob. "That is enough!"

The crowd stopped at this, they'd never been scolded by a politician before. Tilman Bond had never lost his cool, publicly, but at this moment, he was a desperate man.

"Ladies and gentleman, let me remind you that any such stories you may have heard about the history of our town, are unfounded."

Quiet chatter.

"Furthermore, I want to assure you…" he paused, then…"no, I make a vow to you that we will get to the bottom of this. Within the week. We *will* find Tommy Irons and bring him home before the week's end."

He looked down at Tommy's parents, then went on.

"You have my word on that."

Tommy's mother began to cry. The crowd seemed to be satisfied with the mayor's promise. Quietly, they began talking about it amongst themselves.

"Now," Tilman continued, "if I could have all of our volunteers stick around to meet with Sheriff Walker, we'll begin setting up today's search. The rest of you, please, go home. Get some rest. Put these stories out of your mind. Trust that we will take care of this matter."

The crowd, reverently bowed their heads, and began peeling off. Some drifted across the courthouse lawn to continue their conversation. Others left altogether. Storekeepers returned to their shops. Diners retreated back to their tables in the restaurants and sidewalk cafes that framed the square.

Everything casually went back to business as usual.

Mayor Bond turned his back to the crowd and shared a few final words with the city council.

"Mr. Tate, it's nice to see you again," Julia said with a warm smile.

She, along with Bennett and Jordan had been amongst the crowd who came to listen to the mayor's speech.

"Mrs. Taylor, likewise," Max said, extending a handshake.

"I guess Andie found you, alright?" Bennett chimed in.

"Oh, yes, thank you," Max replied.

"When she didn't come back, we figured she must've gone to stay with you," Julia said.

Max stopped dead in his tracks.

So she didn't go back after she left the bar.

"Is something wrong?" Julia asked, reading the expression on Max's face.

"Uh, no. Sorry, I was just…thinking about something else…" he tried to recover.

"Well, tell Andie that we've moved her stuff to the garage. I hope that's OK…but someone else needed to rent the room. Town's full with the search party and all. But she can come by and get it anytime," Julia said with a smile.

Again, Max wandered off for a second, then, coming back to reality,

"Uh, yes, of course. Of course, I will. Thank you…so much."

"Such a shame, isn't it. All of this…" Julia made a sweeping gesture to the almost empty lawn, where the swarming crowd had been only moments ago.

"Yeah, what's that all about?" asked Max.

"Irons boy, disappeared. Just up and vanished," Bennett began.

"He didn't vanish," Julia pleaded, "he's just… missing. Probably ran away. That boy's always been trouble. Skipping school. Smoking pot. Not the kind of kid you'd want hanging around your son."

She gave Jordan a side hug. Max noticed Jordan never looked up. His gaze constantly down at the grass, as if he was trying not to be noticed, as if trying not to be implicated along with Tommy.

"But he'll be found," Julia said. "You heard the mayor. They're pooling the town's resources, even though they're supposed to be focused on *The Festival of Leaves*.

They're doing all they can to bring him home. I know they will. I have faith."

She grabbed the small, golden cross hanging from her necklace.

"Well, we'd better be going," Bennett put a hand on Julia's back.

"You're right," said Julia, looking at her watch. "Bye Mr. Tate, and you be sure and tell Andie…"

"I will," Max said with a fragile smile.

And, just like that, husband, wife, and son quietly left the scene; leaving Max and Sylvia standing alone. Dumbfounded.

"She never went back," Max thought aloud.

"What now?" asked Sylvia. "Is there anyone else in town she knows?"

Max looked over at the gazebo, just as Mayor Bond was descending the steps, making quiet his escape.

"Come on," he insisted.

"Mayor Bond?"

"Mister Tate? I thought we'd agreed that you were leaving town? I'm far too busy to deal with you right now. I've got more pressing matters to attend to."

"Like more disappearances?" Max scoffed.

"Tommy Irons did not disappear, he likely ran away from home. That boy's trouble. But if you tell anyone I said that, I'll—"

"I'm talking about Andie!"

"Andie? I thought you said Ms. Sterling was leaving town with you?"

"Yeah, well, she didn't. And now, it appears she's missing, too. And I think you just might know something about it," Max hissed.

"Just what are you implying?" Sheriff Walker stepped into the discussion.

"Maybe *you* should tell *me*?" Max was growing agitated.

"Mr. Tate, I'm certain I don't know what you're talking about. Like I said, I've got my hands full looking for the Iron's boy," Tilman seethed.

"Mayor Bond?"

Tommy's father caught the mayor's attention.

"Walker, see if you can talk some sense into this man. I have to deal with this," Tilman said, turning away from the conversation.

"Mr. Tate," Walker began, "as you can see, we've got more pressing matters to attend to. Mayor Bond promised that boy's parents we'd find him within the week."

"Could *I* help?" Sylvia approached.

"And you *are*?" Walker asked, annoyed.

"Sylvia Gold..." she paused, "Sylvia Gold. I'm a medium. If you're trying to locate a missing person, I'd love to offer any assistance I can."

"Well, Miss Gold, The Sheriff's Department has all the help they need; *without* your assistance," Walker condescended.

Tilman returned to the conversation.

"Mr. Tate, you're still here."

"If you really want to help," Walker continued.

"If you really wanted to help," Tilman took over, "then you'll get the hell out of this town and stop interfering with our search. Look at us."

Tilman turned to Walker.

"They're already causing us to waste precious time. Let's go, sheriff."

The mayor grabbed Walker by the sleeve and pulled him away.

"Well *that* went well," Sylvia said, sarcastically.

"What was that all about?" Max scorned.

"Excuse me?"

"I'd like to offer my services..." Max threw up a hand, piously, imitating her.

"I thought I might be able to get some more information."

"We're not looking for some teenage boy, we're looking for Andie!"

"Max, did it ever occur to you that the two might be linked?"

Max stopped.

She was right.

Goddamn right.

Once again, he was allowing himself to be so consumed by thoughts of Andie that he was losing sight of the obvious.

This wasn't like Max. He always noticed the details. Except when he allowed himself to get lost thinking about her. Then all logic went out the window. He'd never been like that before. Not ever. But then again, no one else made him feel like Andie. She held some power over him. Maybe Sylvia was right. Maybe Andie was no good for him. Guess it was a good thing that she was here; to keep his head in the game.

"Did you two say that you know Andie Sterling?"

Max turned around to see a woman approaching them. Fashionably dressed and laced in gold and diamond jewelry. She may have been in her late-fifties or early-sixties, yet moved with regal grace, and a youthful energy. She'd either taken good care of herself, or had some work done. Whichever the case, it was obvious that she had the money to do it.

"You know Andie?" Max asked.

"I know *of* her, I'm a fan."

"Have you seen her?" asked Sylvia.

"*Please*, it could be urgent," Max insisted.

"Like I said, I'm just a fan of hers. When I heard she was in town, I wanted to track her down, but then decided against it."

Max's face fell.

"You say she's missing?" the woman continued.

"It seems so," Max said. "And since no one seems to be concerned, we came up here looking for her."

"Have you spoken to the Taylors?" she asked. "I heard she was staying at their place."

"Yes," sighed Sylvia. "We just spoke with them. No help, I'm afraid."

"Was it Julia?" the woman asked.

"Uh, yeah. Why?" asked Max.

The woman paused.

"I figured. You'll never get a straight answer. Not with her around."

She glanced around the square, then pointed toward the East block of shops.

"*Bennett's Coffee Shop*," she continued, "her husband's the owner. He's the one you need to talk to. Or their son, Jordan. Either way, don't talk to Julia."

Before Max could ask why, the woman quietly turned and walked away.

As if she'd never been there.

As if the whole conversation had been in his head.

"God, people in this town are strange," Sylvia laughed. Apparently the bizarre interaction hadn't just been in Max's head *after all*.

"What now?" Sylvia asked.

Max thought for a minute.

"Well, I could go for a cup of coffee. *You*?"

CHAPTER 15

The fragrant aroma of coffee permeated the air. Along with it, the whirling sound of espresso machines and milk steamers frothing away, the clinking of spoons as they stirred about in their ceramic coffee cups, and the soft murmur of jazz hung like a vapor in the background.

Bennett's Coffee Shop was busy for a Saturday afternoon. But, Max assumed that, with the kids out of school for the weekend, this was probably a popular hangout spot for the teens of this town. Each table held a small cluster of people, each engaged in their own conversation, lost in their own private worlds; they floated in the space of the coffee shop like islands scattered in a sea.

"Mr. Tate?" Jordan approached them.

The apron he was wearing suggested that he must work here on the weekends.

"Jordan, isn't it? *Hi*. Do you happen to have any open tables?" Max asked, looking around.

"Sure, right this way."

He took them to a small two top, tucked away in a dark corner of the shop. Industrial-style pendants hung over the tables, the sole source of light, save the sunlight cascading in, through the windows, from the street outside. As such, the room was cast in heavy shadow. A dark atmosphere, further allowing the coffee drinkers to separate themselves from the reality of the outside world. The perfect place for conversation. Max hoped it would serve him in *this* conversation.

"Do you need a moment to look over the menu?" Jordan asked.

"Actually, Jordan, is your dad around? I was hoping to speak with him about something," Max tried to sound very matter-of-fact about it.

"Uh, yeah. Sure. I'll go get him."

"What are you gonna say?" Sylvia asked, once the coast was clear.

"Haven't gotten that far yet," Max replied. "Kinda flying by the seat of my pants here," he laughed.

It's true, he didn't have a plan.

How do you come right out and ask an otherwise perfect stranger if they know something about the woman you love? The one about whom you just lied, saying you know her whereabouts. How do you tell him that you only came into his shop so you could talk to him without his wife around? Something that you only decided you had to do, because some strange lady told you to; a lady that you didn't even bother to ask her name. Maybe she really did know something about Andie's disappearance.

Maybe she had something to do with it. She could've been trying to throw you off her trail for all you know.

The more Max thought about these things, the more stupid he felt. One by one, the clues revealed themselves to be, not only, obvious, but way ahead of him. Clearly, Max was the one who showed up late to this party.

What an idiot.

"Hello again. Jordan said you came in. I'm sorry, I don't think we've officially met," Bennett warmly reached out to shake Sylvia's hand.

"Sylvia Gold. I'm a friend of Andie's. It's nice to

meet you."

"*Bennett*," he said. "The pleasure's all mine. By the way, anything you want is on the house today."

"That's very kind, thank you," Max said.

"Any friend of Andie's is a friend of mine."

Bennett smiled again, even bigger this time. Max could tell that he was a genuine person. Perhaps the first he'd met in this whole damn town.

"So, uh," Bennett went on, "you wanted to speak with me about something?"

Max took a deep breath.

Here goes nothing.

"Yeah. Um, has Andie mentioned anyone in town harassing her? Following her? Anything like that?" Max asked.

Bennett's eyes grew wide.

"No, *why*? Has someone been bothering her?"

"Honestly, we don't know," Max paused, then collected himself. "She, uh, she's gone missing. She was supposed to be back in New York by now, but apparently she never left Hollingshead. We came up here to look for her."

"Jesus," Bennett whispered to himself. "I was afraid something like this might happen."

"You knew she was in trouble?" Sylvia asked.

Bennett looked around, then leaned in.

"She's been going around town, asking a lot of questions."

"Yeah, so?" Max replied.

"You don't get it. The people in this town...they don't like to bring up the past. They'll do whatever it takes—" Bennett's words trailed off as he got lost in his thoughts.

His face was ashen. Then he quietly slipped back into the conversation.

"I was worried about her. Told her to keep her head down, stop talking to folks around town. Even *I* thought I was being too paranoid, ya know? Like that kind of thing only happens in the movies. Guess this town *really is* that fucked up."

Max and Sylvia looked at each other. This time Sylvia began.

"Will you help us, Bennett?"

"How?"

"Tell us what you know. What is it about this town—"

"No!" Bennett whispered, sharply. "I mean, I will do whatever I can, but not *that*. I've got my family to think about. You don't know how long it took me to find a place in this town. You don't know what it means that I finally fit in *here*. I'm not going to risk giving up all of that. Putting my family in harm's way…"

Max didn't wanna push him; not now.

Not, *yet*.

They'd only just arrived…there was more digging that they could do alone. Bennett was an asset, and likely a friend. They needed to wait to play that card as a last resort.

"We understand," Max sympathized. "We wouldn't want you to put your family in any danger. If there's anything else you can think about that might be helpful to us, a name, a place, anything that might point us in the right direction, you will let us know, won't you?"

"Of course."

Bennett pulled out a business card and placed it on the table in front of Max.

"My contact info's all here. If you find something, please, don't hesitate."

Max gave him an affirming nod. Bennett responded with the like, then knocked his knuckles on the table, bidding them farewell, then made his way back to the counter.

"Now what?" Sylvia asked.

Max looked at his watch. It was after three o'clock,

now. At least they could check into the hotel.

"C'mon. Let's go. We'll get settled into our rooms, clean up a bit, then we can make a game plan for this evening."

At first Sylvia almost protested, I mean why waste more time? But then she decided he was right. She was so tired from the flight and long drive up here, that her senses weren't really picking up on anything. Some time alone, away from everyone, including Max, would be just the thing she needed to recharge.

"Alright, *Casanova*. Let's get the hell outta here," she grinned.

Before they left, Max did two things.

First, he added Bennett as a contact into his phone.

Second, he changed the wallpaper of his phone to a photo of Andie; if they were gonna go around town asking folks if they'd seen her, it was easier to just have her photo on-hand at all times. This morning hadn't been as fruitful as either of them had hoped; but at least they were here.

At least it was a start.

CHAPTER 16

"Yes, Mr. and Mrs. Tate, I have you down for one, King room. Does that sound right?" the hotel clerk was too busy looking at his computer screen to even look up at them.

"Uh, no..."

Sylvia pushed herself in front of Max, spreading herself across the counter in a desperate attempt to look intimidating. She went on.

"First of all, we're *not* together, I mean, we are, but, not like *that*. He wishes..."

"Excuse me?" Max chimed in.

"Secondly, we are going to need *TWO* rooms. Preferably non-adjoining rooms, but a girl can't be too picky, I suppose."

"Well, ma'am, I do apologize," the clerk began, "but I'm afraid that's just not possible."

"Not possible? My reservation clearly says two rooms," Max said.

"Yes, sir, and again I do apologize. But with town being so busy, first, with, *The Festival of Leaves*, then all of the volunteers that came to town and join in the search party for that missing boy, I'm afraid this one room is likely the *only* room left available in the entire town."

"Well, then, I'll just have to take the room and you can sleep in the car," Sylvia said, turning to Max.

"What about a roll-away bed? Do you have those?" Max asked the clerk.

"Oh *no*, you're *not* suggesting we sleep in the same room—"

"Sylvia, *not now*," Max cut her off, annoyed.

"None available," the clerk apologized, "but the room does have a sofa. Not a sofa-bed, but you'll be plenty comfortable."

"That'll make one of us," Sylvia murmured under her breath.

Max shot her an irritated glance.

"Fine, we'll take it," he said.

Max displayed his driver's license, then swiped his credit card for the incidentals. When the clerk was telling them about the elevators and the location of the ice machine, Max's phone rang. He excused himself, and stepped to the side, as Sylvia finished up at the desk.

"Ray? Thank god, you don't know how happy I am to hear from you."

Yeah, Max couldn't believe the words coming out of his mouth, either. I mean, Ray annoyed him even more than Sylvia. But, with no viable leads to go on, surely Ray had something for them. Max hadn't told him about Andie's disappearance. Instead he chose to focus more on the history of the town and how they were having trouble getting the locals to cooperate in their investigation. As far as Ray knew, that's why Max had gone to Hollingshead.

"Maxi-pad!" Ray laughed at his own joke, *typical.* "Have I used that one before?"

"No, uh, I don't think so…good one."

Max faked a laugh.

Come on you sonofabitch, enough of the bullshit. Gimme something useful.

"Alright, alright. On to business. I've got the names of two people you need to talk to; locals who know things and are willing to talk."

Max opened the notes app on his phone.

"OK, shoot."

"The first is a guy by the name of Peter McManus. But apparently the locals call him *Crazy Pete*. He's locked up in some mental hospital, just on the edge of town, called *Evergreen Pointe*."

"*Great, a lunatic,*" Max thought aloud.

Although, he was chasing after a girl who, by her own admission didn't want him, and he'd enlisted the help of some eccentric, middle-aged psychic to help in his quest, so maybe he was pretty near certifiable, himself.

"And the second?" asked Max.

"Eleanor Bond. She's married to the mayor of Hollingshead. Family goes all the way back to the founding members of the town. Fucking family has ran that town since day one. If you wanna know anything, she's the one to ask."

"Goddamn. I owe you one, man," Max replied.

"More than you know, man," Ray chuckled, "more than you know…"

*****

That night, in his hotel room, Max dreamed again. He dreamed of the monstrous house, sitting upon its lush meadow, overlooking the sea; at least what was left of it. The charred ruins, now the skeleton of what once had been. Its walls and windows were drawn back, exposing the guts of the house. Black mounds of ash lay within, concealing all but the occasional pulse of red, glowing embers.

The sky was black. No moon. No stars. All was quiet. Deadly quiet. The screaming had stopped, the flames had died out, and all that remained was a small campfire, across the lawn from the house. A campfire which served to protect both mother and daughter from the chill of the night, while providing enough light to help spot intruders.

Next to the fire, Bella slept. Still in her pink dress. Her golden hair now wringed with sweat, from the hours spent next to the unbridled blaze. Her pure, lily white skin now tainted with streaks of ash and soot. But, for the moment, peace enveloped her, as she slept quietly by; without a care in the world.

The same could not be said for the girl's mother, Camilla. The dark woman sat on the opposite side of the fire, watching the child. Her eyes were sore and pestered by the remains of dried tears. Her ears still ringing with the sounds of the screams and cries of all the poor souls locked inside the towering inferno. She could still hear them. Their pain. Their fear. Their anguish. The very thought made her sick to her stomach. She covered her ears with her hands and closed her eyes tightly to block out the noise; but it didn't help.

Worse still, she knew that she was responsible for all of it. All of these people died because of her. Sure, she hadn't been the one to lock the doors and set fire to the house, but she might as well have. In her ignorance, she had brainwashed the child. Manipulated her, all in hopes that the child would choose her, over the parents who'd raised her.

If all of that weren't enough, she feared for the child. For her soul. Surely, this child was damned. No amount of penance, no degree of atonement could clear her sins. She had the blood of countless, innocent souls on her hands. And for that, surely she'd have to pay; for all eternity.

Or did she?

A thought struck Camilla at once.

She closed her eyes and looked deep within herself for an answer. Yes, she knew what she'd do.

It would work.

It *had* to work.

She knelt close to the fire and scooped up a handful of dirt from the ground. With it safely in her grasp, she drew it to her lips and whispered into it. Then, after a moment of hesitation, threw the dirt into the fire.

Immediately, the blaze erupted into a fierce, smoldering column. Black plumes of smoke stretched all the way up to the cold, granite sky. None of this disturbed the sleeping child.

The woman took in a deep breath, then began speaking in a strange tongue, her eyes rolled back into their sockets and her eyelids fluttered frantically as she became lost in a trance. Kneeling in front of the flames, she hinged at the waist and rocked about, like a gyroscope.

A figure appeared before her, wrapped in the flames. It may've been man, based on its faint features, or it may not have been human at all. Whatever it was, it was horrific. Initially, it didn't speak, it only listened as Camilla pleaded her case. Still speaking in her strange language, she fell upon the ground, burying her face in the dirt, pounding her fists upon the earth, and begging the thing for something.

Uninterested in what she had to say, the thing began to fade back into the flames. Her face became even more desperate. She looked over at Bella and began to weep.

That's when it came to her.

An idea.

Something she knew that the creature couldn't refuse.

She shouted for it to return. It did. She directed the conversation in the direction of the girl. Frantically, she pointed and gestured, speaking so quickly that she couldn't possibly have taken the time to think about what she was saying, what she was promising the beast.

When she was done, she dropped her hands and waited. Desperately out of breath, still shaking from her desperate proposal, wondering if it was all in vain. The thing was silent. Contemplating the matter.

Then, finally, it let out a terrifying roar that shook the very ground like an earthquake. The flames twisted and writhed like a massive thicket, shooting up, and up, and up. The woman threw herself back, terrified.

And, in an instant, it was over. All was quiet and calm just as before. The woman still on one side of the small campfire, and the child, still sleeping safe and sound, on the other. Blissfully unaware that anything had happened.

Was it all over?

Would the bargain be worth the price?

The woman didn't know.

She wouldn't know.

But, for now, all was as it should be.

The child, was safe.

THE HAND THAT FEEDS YOU

What was that?

Camilla heard something. A low rumble. The ground seemed to be vibrating. Then she saw something, a flash of light moved amongst the trees in the dense forest-which encircled the far half of the estate. A forest that had once felt like a barricade, protecting them from the outside world, was now feeling more like a cage which served to trap them in.

The rumble grew louder, it was the sound of footsteps, an army of men and horses. Then came the shouting. The woman shrieked in terror, as the party emerged from the trees. Probably a hundred of them. Men on horseback, others on foot, some holding weapons, others flaming torches. All wearing a look of revenge upon their faces.

"Come on, Doniă. We must go…now," she awoke the girl, scooping her up in her arms.

She wanted to run. To find a place of safety, but it was too late. Besides, where could she go? The forest was too far away, and she'd have to cross through the mob to get to it. Behind her was the edge of the cliff. It was hopeless.

"There's the witch! Get her!" shouted one of the men. Moving as one, the army invaded the meadow, sweeping ruthlessly across the landscape, closing in on the woman and the girl.

Knowing there was nothing she could do, Camilla stood there, awaiting her fate.

"She's got a child!" cried one of the men.

"Grab it from her!" commanded another.

Bella was ripped from her mother's arms, as Camilla helplessly screamed in protest.

"Bind her hands and feet!"

The men shouted and cheered.

"Throw the witch into the sea!"

They drew ropes around her wrists and ankles, pulling them until they drew blood. The girl watched, safely from the arms of one of the men; although she cried and pleaded with them to stop.

"There, there, child. It'll all be over soon. She's not gonna hurt you anymore," said the man, tenderly.

The girl couldn't understand why these men were doing this to her mother. When her cries became too much, one of the men ordered her to be taken away from the scene.

"The poor child shouldn't have to see this," he insisted.

And with that, she was scooped up and carried away from the horrific scene.

One of the men opened a large canvas bag, while a

handful of others began filling it with large stones. When the bottom of the bag was sufficiently filled, they placed the woman on top of the stone pile, then began sewing up the bag.

Amidst her cries, Camilla made one last attempt to gain vengeance upon her aggressors. Reciting her words in that strange tongue once more, first in a low murmur, then louder, and louder, and louder, until she was shouting at the top of her lungs. Her voice echoed across the expanse of the clearing, then rolled down the chasm; challenging the turbulent waves of the roaring sea.

As if in response to her words, her strange spell, a dense, dark fog sinisterly rolled across the terrain. Low and faint, at first, then it grew thicker, grew darker. It rose higher and higher, until it engulfed the entire house, the clearing, and everyone around it. All was lost in its wake. The men began coughing and choking.

"I can't see!"

"I can't breathe!"

"No! Do not give in!" one of them shouted.

"Let's kill this witch! She must be stopped!"

With the woman securely sealed up inside, a group of men lifted the bag, and carried it towards the edge of the cliff.

Overwhelmed by the dense fog, they lost track of the ground beneath them and before they could stop themselves, a string of them fell off the edge of the cliff, taking the woman with them. Some fell into the sea, others were splattered across the jagged rocks below. Whether ready, or not, each went on to meet their maker in the blink of an eye. Each just one more casualty of the cursed estate.

Then, silence. Suddenly everything was as it had been before. Well almost everything. The fog had lifted and the sky was now clear. For the first time tonight, a brilliant moon smiled upon those who remained, while a million stars congratulated them for victoriously surviving their crusade.

Strangely, though, the ruins of the great house were gone. The only evidence of what had been there before was the small campfire, popping cheerily against the crisp sea breeze.

The men stood silent. Trying to compose themselves.
Trying to gather their thoughts.
Trying to make sense of all they'd just witnessed.

CHAPTER 17

The next morning, Max and Sylvia headed down to *Bennett's Coffee* for breakfast. This would become their daily ritual while in Hollingshead. They'd discuss thoughts that came to them during the night, plan the course of the day, and do their best to convince each other (and themselves) that they'd find Andie, safe and sound; something that was getting more and more difficult as the days went by.

Max still hadn't told Sylvia about the dreams, last night's was no exception. He just couldn't bring himself to do it. He wanted to talk to someone about them, try and gain some insight as to their meaning, or why he was having them in the first place. But, telling Sylvia meant that he'd be subject to odious amounts of mumbo jumbo. He could just hear her now, *the spirits are at work! They're speaking to you! You've opened a portal! Blah, blah, blah.* Yeah, he wasn't desperate enough to open that door; not yet anyway.

"How'd you sleep?" she asked, taking a sip of her hot tea.

"Fine," he lied. "You?"

"Same as every other night in this forsaken town… with my hands between my legs."

Both of them laughed. Lighthearted moments like this were a welcomed retreat from the gloomy reality of their cause.

"Busy day, today…" he began, "I'm all set to interview Peter McManus at ten. Really wish I could go with you to interview the mayor's wife, but Peter's doctor was kind enough to let me in to see him, and I didn't wanna risk losing that invitation by rescheduling."

"Divide and conquer," she said. "Eh, we'll cover more ground that way, *anyway*. Better use of our time."

"I guess," Max feigned.

"See? I told you you'd need me to come along."

As much as he hadn't wanted her to tag along, initially, he had to admit, he was warming up to her; psychic shit and all.

*****

"Mr. Tate?" the woman extended a solid handshake.

"*Max*."

"Dr. Sharma. I'm Peter's psychiatrist," she released his hand.

"I really can't thank you enough for this."

"Anything for a friend of Ray's," she smiled.

Max laughed, nervously.

"What are the odds that a friend of Ray's is the doctor at this very hospital? Or even more so that we all went to college together?"

"Go *Devils*," she said, triumphantly holding up the sign of the horns.

"Go *Devils*," he responded with the like, "small world."

"Smaller than you know. How *is* Ray?"

"Still talking non-stop."

"Same old Ray," laughed the doctor.

"So, what can you tell me about Peter?" asked Max, getting down to business.

"He prefers Pete. And, due to *HIPAA* laws, not much, I'm afraid."

She began walking down a corridor, lined with

evenly-spaced doors, each had a long, rectangular window hung in its center. Max trailed behind her.

"To be honest," she continued, "I'm not sure how much you'll be able to get from him, either."

"Why's that?"

"Well, in the last three years, I think I've only heard him say maybe two or three words."

"He doesn't talk?"

"He can, he just chooses not to. In the sixty-some years he's been here every doctor who's treated him has had similar experiences."

"Is he violent?" Max asked.

He knew Pete had been sentenced to this asylum in lieu of prison, after he was tried for the disappearance of his friend in the nineteen sixties.

"No," said the doctor. "He doesn't really show *any* emotion, he just seems to...exist."

She stopped at one of the doors where a woman in scrubs was standing guard. Then turned to Max.

"Max, this is Michelle, Pete's nurse. She'll be in the room with you if you need anything. I'll be watching from the observation room on the other side of the mirror."

The doctor gave both of them an affirming nod, then

she was gone.

"Are you ready?" asked the nurse.

Max took in a deep breath.

"Let's see what happens."

The room was sterile. Not unpleasant, or uncomfortable, just sterile. The walls were painted a drab shade of beige, the carpet was that forgettable type of industrial Berber, and the only furnishings were a heavy, wooden table, and three stackable chairs. One for each of them.

"Pete? You have a visitor. This is Mr. Tate. He wants to ask you a few questions. Does that sound alright?"

No response.

"OK, Mr. Tate. He's all yours," she said.

She then retreated to the chair against the wall in the far corner of the room; leaving Max alone in his own little world with Pete. *Crazy Pete.*

The man looked so fragile. He was almost eighty, but it wasn't the years that had aged him…it was, well, Max couldn't quite pin just what it was. He had wispy strands of snowy hair, wrapping the outer parameter of his head; to Max, it resembled a laurel crown.

His gaunt face was expressionless. Emotionless. Rigid

features littered his facade, befitting of a wise old man. A sage, in The Hero's Journey, were he to be cast according to type. Yet, that was a role he'd never get to play, because, as the doctor had accurately pointed out, he merely existed. For the first time, Max regretted following Ray's lead. Maybe he should've rescheduled, risked losing this interview, then he could've gone with Sylvia to see the mayor's wife. That was a bigger fish to fry.

"Hi, Pete. Can I call you *Pete*?"

Silence.

"I heard you like to read comic books."

Max opened up his messenger bag, and placed a few superhero comics on the table, in front of Pete.

"Look, Pete, it's *Superman*. Your favorite," the nurse said, leaning forward from her chair.

Still, nothing.

She leaned back into position, and shrugged her shoulders, as if to say *I tried*. As if to say *I told you so*.

Max was really feeling sorry for himself now, this was his only "*in*" with the patient, something he was assured would pique Pete's interest; but the poor guy just sat there, staring off in the distance. Perhaps reliving the moments when he was normal. Reliving the life he'd once lived, before this became his reality.

Max leaned back in his chair, sizing up the situation. He knew where he wanted to go with the conversation, but he didn't know how to start. Who knew if he'd even get a word outta the guy? But, he'd have to try. After all, Ray had thrown him this lead, and Ray was never wrong.

"Pete," Max began, "I hear that you and a friend went hiking up the coast."

The nurse sat up at this, glaring at Max. Clearly he was talking about a taboo topic. But, still, Pete didn't react. Not in the slightest.

"Is that true?" Max continued. "Did you see something up there? Did your friend see something up there?"

Max's eyes were engaged in a ping-pong match after each question-from the nurse to see if he was going to be cut-off, to Pete, to see if he'd struck a nerve.

Maybe a visual will help, he thought.

Max pulled out his phone, opened that infamous email that Andie had gotten, luring her to come to Maine. He opened the attachment, the photo of the burned house.

"Does this look familiar?"

He held up the phone.

No response, of course.

But, Pete hadn't even looked at it.

Give me something, you crazy sonofabitch.

"Have you ever seen this house, Pete?"

Max placed the phone directly in front of the man's gaze, *no refusing to look at it now.*

In an instant, Pete jumped to his feet and began swinging his hands in defense of the image; smacking Max's phone to the floor.

"That's quite enough, Mr. Tate," the nurse stepped into frame, casting an icy glance at Max.

He knew it was intrusive, but he was desperate; might as well shoot his shot, rather than completely waste his day.

The nurse worked to calm her patient, and Max was certain her next course of action was to escort him out to the room, perhaps calling security to escort him from the hospital; but, then…

"Shrouded in darkness…" Pete's words were barely more than a whisper, uttered more to himself as if recalling something he'd been told.

"What's that? What's shrouded in darkness?" Max implored.

"I didn't hurt him…" Pete said.

He looked Max directly in the eye.

"The house *did*."

Max regained his seat, across the table and leaned in to keep the conversation going. The nurse did the same, taking up a position next to Pete.

"You've seen this house? Where? When? Was it that night?" Max was trying not to bombard the fragile guy, but he couldn't help himself. Finally, someone knew something about this mystery.

"Seb and I were drinking beer in the woods. We'd both snuck out of our houses. We did that sometimes, small town, not much to do..." Pete's voice trailed off.

"And? What happened next?" Max brought him back to reality.

"There was a woman. A beautiful woman. Never seen her before. She asked us for a drink. So, we gave her one. And the three of us talked and talked."

"And this woman, did she tell you about the house?" Max persisted.

"She said there was a treasure. Said it was buried in an old house up the coast. Supposed to be haunted, but she'd been there. Said she'd take us there, and if we found the treasure, we'd split it three ways."

Max kept glancing at the door, wondering when Dr. Sharma might come in and interrupt this interrogation.

"So, you went to the house?" asked Max.

"It was dark. Foggy. Could barely see a thing. We almost got lost in the woods, but then, sure enough, we found it. It was monstrous. I didn't wanna go in. Had second thoughts after seeing it in-person. But, she was persistent, we had to go inside to find the treasure. Seb was so taken with her, I knew he'd do *anything* she said. So, we went inside."

Pete closed his eyes tightly.

Max could see him playing out those experiences in real-time.

"Pete? Are you there? What are you seeing?"

"I see…I see…"

He opened his eyes, which were red and en-wrapped with tears.

"Terrible things."

"Pete, I know you're afraid, but can you tell me, please…" Max begged.

"I got scared, so I ran out of the house, and when I turned around…the house…it…disappeared," he looked resolutely at Max, once more, "Seb was still, trapped inside."

Just then, Max's phone, which was sitting on the

table, received a text alert, causing its screen to light up.

Pete looked down at the phone's screen and became irate once more. This time, he was incorrigible. He ran from the phone, threw himself into a fetal position on the floor and kept screaming,

"No! Go Away! No!"

Dr. Sharma came bursting into the room, as the nurse scooped Pete off the floor, and quickly administered a sedative injection.

The man instantly calmed down, as if nothing had happened. Max wondered what was in that pen, and if he could get a dose or two for the road.

"Take him to his room, please," said the doctor, "I'll be there shortly."

The nurse helped her patient to his feet, then gingerly escorted him out of the room; closing the door behind them.

"What did you show him?" the doctor threw an accusatory look at Max.

He opened the photo of the house.

"This was the first photo I showed him."

"And the second?"

He went to his home screen. It was a photo of Andie. The one he'd set as his wallpaper to help expedite the process of asking locals if they'd seen her. Was that what had scared Pete?

Maybe she'd come to see him, too.

Max held up his phone.

"Do you recognize this woman? Maybe she's paid a visit to Pete, recently?"

"No. You're the first visitor he's had since I've been here. Is she your girlfriend?"

Max's stomach sank.

"No, just, a *friend*."

"Well, you've been able to get more out of him than anyone who's treated him. That's impressive."

"Do you know anything about this house?" Max asked.

"Nothing, really. People talk, but you can't take any of it seriously."

I'm starting to think you can, he thought.

"What about his friend, Seb? The one who disappeared? You think Pete had something to do with his disappearance?"

"Well, like I said, earlier, I'm unable to discuss him at length with anyone who isn't family."

"But, you did say you didn't think he was violent,"

Max began, "what about all of that? Seems to me like he could've done something—"

"He was frightened, Max."

The doctor thought for a moment, choosing her words carefully. Then,

"I will say this, I don't know the specifics of what he's been through, but I know it had to be something pretty traumatic, something bad. Everyone responds to trauma differently. He's chosen to shut down, to lock it all away. But, whenever you showed him those photos, you forced him to relive that trauma. In that moment, he was right back there, face to face with whatever he'd seen...whatever he'd *tried* to forget."

CHAPTER 18

Max had taken an *Uber* to the hospital, leaving Sylvia in town with the car. Letting her drive his car was something he didn't exactly feel too good about, but it seemed to make the most sense. Turns out, he had good reason to worry. The native New Yorker hadn't sat behind the steering wheel since a rather tumultuous Driver's Ed course, in high school, on Long Island. Max went ahead and sprang for the extra coverage insurance, when he rented the car at the airport; just in case such an opportunity were to present itself.

The *Volvo* skirted about the narrow streets of downtown. Rolling through stop signs and brushing up against curbs that had to've been placed there by mistake, according to Sylvia. Eventually, and mostly unscathed, it reached its destination, the office of Eleanor Bond.

Mayor's Wife, or even First Lady had to be a diminutive title for her. Turns out, Eleanor did just a little bit of everything around this town. So much that she needed a business office, complete with a personal assistant to handle all of her daily scheduling and minor errand running. Located in the historic business district, the office building was juxtaposed to its surroundings. The original building, like all of its neighbors, had been constructed in the mid-eighteen hundreds, but renovated within the last few years. Now, with the original facade still visible and intact, it was wrapped in a mixture of steel and tempered glass. A taste of SoHo in this sleepy little town of whimsical bed and breakfasts.

"I'm here to see Ms. Bond," Sylvia did her best to mask her thick, New York accent.

The chic assistant looked up at her, trying equally as hard to mask her snide chuckle at the woman's eclectic wardrobe, messy jewelry, and at least five pounds of heavy-handed makeup.

"And you have an appointment?"

"No, I'm sorry, I don't. But, it's very, very important."

"I'm sure," the assistant rolled her eyes, "Mrs. Bond

can see you, sometime next week. Thursday or Friday?"

"No, I need to see her today! The sooner the better, *please*."

Sylvia tried her best not to sound too anxious, even though she *was*. With the way the snooty assistant looked at her, keeping her cool was the one shred of dignity she had left.

"I'm sorry, who'd you say you were?"

"Sylvia, Sylvia Gold, and you are?"

Sylvia extended a handshake, which the assistant sneered at, but did not return.

"I am…afraid that's just not possible."

"If you'll just tell her, it's an emergency—"

"Even if I wanted to, *which I don't*, Mrs. Bond is out of the office today. And I am very busy, taking care of things with her gone."

"If you'll just tell me where I can find—"

"So, I'm going to get back to work, and you can…go back to the parking lot of some truck-stop, or whatever thrift store shamefully sold you that hideous ensemble. Good day to you."

The assistant picked up the phone and started dialing.

Sylvia felt herself tearing up at the insult, but, again,

she'd vowed to maintain her dignity.

"And to you as well," she said, turning to leave.

When she got to the door, she overheard the assistant talking on the phone.

"Hi, Amaury. I'm just letting you know that Mrs. Bond is canceling her reservation today. That's right, she'll be having lunch at the country club."

Then I'll head to the country club, Sylvia thought to herself.

✱✱✱✱✱

The *GPS* took her right to the parking lot.

Since she had no idea who she was looking for, she decided to sit on a bench, near the entrance, where she wouldn't be noticed by the doorman.

Sylvia wasn't country club material, she knew this, but she also delighted in it. These people were entitled, self-important, and fake; something she wasn't.

Except, maybe she *was*.

As she sat there, watching an endless parade of overpriced khaki and cashmere enter and exit the pretentious, brick building; listening to them being lauded by name, as they arrived or departed, she wondered if she were as misguided as they were.

Nearly her entire life, she'd spent preaching the power of the fates, the wisdom of the cosmos, the definitive proof of the spirit world; herself being a messenger for it. But, here she was, at a time when it really mattered, a time when she needed to call upon her abilities to save a friend, and she had felt nothing. The main reason she was so insistent that she come with Max to Maine was that she was certain she'd feel Andie's presence. If Andie was still here, Sylvia would know it. She'd *feel* it, deep within her, just like she had with all of the others she'd helped over the years. But, she didn't feel anything here. What did that mean? Did it mean that Andie had left town? Or worse, that she was *dead*? Or did it mean that Max was right? Maybe Sylvia was nothing more than a fraud; a fraud who'd bought the lies she'd spun over the years. *Was that possible?*

No, it couldn't be.

Could it?

"Have a good day, Mr. and Mrs. Bond."

The doorman bowed to the couple as they descended the front steps. Sylvia collected herself, then went after the fleeting couple.

"Mrs. Bond?" Sylvia called out.

No sooner had the woman turned around, Sylvia

stopped dead in her tracks. She knew this woman; well, she didn't know her, but she'd seen her that very first day when they'd arrived in town. Mrs. Bond was the woman who'd directed them to speak to Bennett, away from Julia.

"Do you know this woman?" Tilman asked, turning to his wife.

"Uh, no, I'm afraid I don't," she said, confused.

"It's Sylvia Gold. We spoke a few days ago. I'm a friend of Andie Sterling."

Eleanor's face winced.

"Andie Sterling?! You went to meet with Andie Sterling?!"

Tilman sounded furious.

"*No!*" Eleanor protested.

"After we specifically agreed you wouldn't—" he continued.

"Tilman, darling," she turned her husband to face her, placed both hands tenderly on his chest and began working her magic on him, "I told you I wouldn't and I didn't. I don't know this woman and I don't know what she's talking about."

Both of them turned to look at Sylvia, who was both confused and unsure what to do next.

"Miss, Gold, was it?" Tilman condescended, "it appears you are mistaken. My wife says she doesn't know you, and if you're a friend of Miss Sterling, well then I'm certain you have no business being here. As I've already told Mr. Tate, on multiple occasions, you are not welcome here. If you know what's best for you, you'll both pack your things and go. Post Haste!"

"But if you'll just let me—" Sylvia tried to say.

"Get the hell out of my town!"

Tilman's voice was so thunderous that everyone outside the club was staring at them now, he finished the blow with,

"The next time I won't be so friendly about it."

Broken, and disheartened, Sylvia collapsed into herself, turned around, and walked back to her car.

Sure. She may've been a fraud, but she wasn't cruel like these people.

Good riddance.

✻✻✻✻✻

Max was already waiting for Sylvia at their usual table at the coffee shop. They'd agreed to meet up after their respective interviews to exchange information, debrief, and plan their next move.

He excitedly told her about Pete, and the bizarre way he'd reacted to the photos. While neither of them could say, with any certainty, exactly what that all meant, it did mean that they were on the right track.

When it was her turn, Sylvia quickly extinguished Max's excitement about Eleanor, by giving him a play-by-play of her day. The only redeeming factor was that Eleanor was the woman they'd met on the lawn of the town square. So, why did she deny knowing them? What was she hiding? Maybe she did have something to do with Andie's disappearance and she was trying to throw them off her scent. That was an option they'd have to explore.

"Would you like your usual?" Jordan asked them with that familiar, shy smile.

"Unless you've got something stronger than coffee." Max said.

After the blow about Eleanor, he could use a hard drink.

"I can make it a triple shot," Jordan laughed.

"Deal," Max nodded.

"And what would you like, Ms. Gold?"

Sylvia shot him a look that went right through him.

"You know what I'd like Jordan? I'd like for you to

tell me about the thirteen missing, or maybe the million secrets they're buried under."

"Uh, huh?" Jordan stammered.

"Sylvia," Max began, "what are you—"

"Or tell me about this house, huh, *Jordan*? Do you know anything about *it*?"

She practically threw her phone in his face. As soon as his eyes saw the picture, he looked away, nervously.

"That's enough Sylvia, he's just a kid, you can't—"

"Or, at least, tell us why you sent Andie that email, and now you won't even talk about it!"

All three went silent for a moment, then,

"You? You sent the email, Jordan?" Max inquired. "*Why*?"

Jordan looked at Max, apologetically. Then at Sylvia.

"We're waiting, Jordan? Or do I need to ask you dad about it? Or maybe…your mom?" Sylvia persisted.

"No!" Jordan shouted in a stifled whisper.

He paused for a moment, looked around, then thought about it for a moment. After drawing in a long, deep breath,

"Fine, I'll tell you," he said, leaning into the table. "But not here, not now…come back after closing. I'll be done by nine fifteen or nine twenty; can't hurry out or my dad'll get suspicious. Meet me outside. I'll tell you everything."

Then, he was gone. Max sat there, bewildered.

First of all, *Jordan* had sent the email that had prompted Andie to come here? That shy kid? Of all people, he was the *last* person Max would've suspected.

Secondly,

"How the hell did *you* know that?" he asked her in utter disbelief.

He was used to being the first to figure these things out. But, this? There were no signs. Zero. Nothing that suggested Jordan was the guilty one.

Sylvia looked upset that he'd say something like this. She sat back in her chair, folded her arms, then,

"You're impossible, you know that?" she scoffed.

"What?"

"No matter how much time we've spent together, no matter how many times I tell you that I'm a psychic, tell you about all of my experiences, my abilities, and still you refuse to accept that maybe, *just maybe*, it's all true!"

He felt small.

He wasn't sure what it was about her tone that cut right through him. He also couldn't pinpoint why she was bringing this up, now; but she *was* right. A week ago, he never would've considered it. He'd never believed in anything that he couldn't see. But, the nightmares, the strange feeling he got just being in this bizarre town, the look of fear in Pete's eyes when he talked about that house...clearly *something* was affecting this town and everyone in it.

If such dark forces actually *did* exist, then who's to say that Sylvia couldn't actually be telling the truth?

After all, that made more sense than her figuring out that Jordan had sent that email, before he could.

"I'm sorry. You're right..." Max said.

"I am?"

Max sighed, hard. This wasn't an easy thing to say.

"Sylvia," he gently placed a hand on hers, "you know I'm a skeptic, and you know I have my reasons. Still, that doesn't make it right to belittle you or your...abilities. The things I've witnessed since coming to this town, the things I've...felt...well, they tell me that maybe I don't know as much as I thought I did. Maybe, just maybe, there is some truth to what you do."

She was dumbfounded, she'd never expected him to change his stance on that, but in her moment of self-doubt, it sure felt nice that someone believed in her.

"So you're saying you believe?"

"I'm saying," he paused, "I'm saying that there's a possibility."

He gave a weak smile. Sylvia, on the other hand, was beaming.

"Thank you," she said, before picking up his hand to kiss it.

"Now you're the one getting fresh," Max said with a laugh, jerking his hand away.

They both laughed.

Another, welcomed, moment of laughter.

"Oh," Sylvia said, "before I forget to tell you, your friend Ray called the hotel today. He said he tried texting you, but you never responded."

Must've been the text that set Pete off at the hospital, Max thought.

"What'd he want?"

"He just wanted to tell you that he'd traced back the sender of that email, that Andie'd received. Turns out, it came from a student account at *Hollingshead High School*, under the user name: *jordan.taylor08*."

They sat there for a second.

Then, *laughter*.

"Sonofabitch!" Max laughed.

"But I got you to admit it! You're a believer!" Sylvia said, laughing so hard that she could barely speak.

*****

That evening, at nine twenty three, Jordan walked out the front door of the coffee shop, locked up, and spotted Max and Sylvia waiting outside of Max's car. The three of them casually climbed in, Max and Sylvia up front, and Jordan in the back.

"So?" Max began, "are you gonna tell us what you know?"

"I'll tell you on two conditions," Jordan said, hesitantly.

"Which are?" Max asked.

"First, what I'm about to tell you, you can't tell anyone. Deal?"

Max and Sylvia looked at each other, uncertain. They may be listening to a murder confession for all they knew.

"I'm not sure we can promise that, but I can promise you that we'll do our best," Max reassured, "and? What's the second condition?"

Jordan stared down at the space of leather car seat, between his knees.

Gaining the courage to speak, then,

THE HAND THAT FEEDS YOU

"The second is,"

He looked up at them, his eyes wide with fear,

"You can't think I'm crazy."

CHAPTER 19

The screeching of tires, furious rubber at odds with the asphalt trying to hold it back, echoed through the streets of town.

"Max! Slow down!" Sylvia pleaded with him.

But it was useless, he was going to extract as much energy as he possibly could from those eight cylinders. Outside the car windows, the view quickly shifted from city blocks, and dimly-lit streets, to the dark, unforgiving road that stretched along the desolate coast.

"Is this the road?!" Max's voice was demanding.

"Yeah," came a murmur from the backseat.

"Jordan, why don't you tell us again?" Sylvia asked.

If Max was the throttle, Sylvia was the brake. Her voice was calm and reassuring. She was going to try a different approach to extract all that she could from the boy.

"But I already told you everything, I swear!"

"Just in case we missed something, please? You said that you and Tommy Irons were waiting outside of the bar that night, when Andie went to meet Max?"

"Yeah—"

"Why didn't you tell the police?!" Max demanded.

"Because they'd think I did it!" Jordan shot back. "I mean, as far as I know, I was the last one to see either of them, alive."

"What were you doing outside the bar?" Sylvia redirected the conversation.

"We were in my truck, smoking pot."

"Were you stalking her?" Max veered a bit too close to the edge, then regained the center of the road.

"No! God, no. I'd told Tommy that she was staying with us, he said there was no way that a girl that hot was staying at our house. I knew she was going to meet you there, so I drove there and waited outside to prove him wrong."

"What happened then? After you saw her?" Sylvia asked.

"She got in her car to leave, and Tommy said he wanted to follow her. See where she went. At first I didn't want to, but then I saw she was going back up this road, and since it was storming again, I thought, maybe it was a good idea; in case she got stuck again."

"Turn here?" Max asked, as they passed an intersecting road.

"No, you just keep going straight."

"OK, so you boys followed her up here," Sylvia continued.

"Probably high outta your minds," snapped Max.

"That's enough out of you," Sylvia snapped back.

"I'm just saying, they weren't thinking straight, could've done something they'd regret later," Max looked at him in the rear-view mirror.

"No! That's not true! We didn't—"

"Lookout!" Sylvia yelled, just as Max slammed on his brakes.

"This is the place. This is where we parked the truck," Jordan exhaled.

There they were, sitting face to face with the monstrous boulder; missing it by mere centimeters.

"There's the spot Andie drove her car in," Jordan pointed to an innocuous bare patch in the dense array of rugged pine trees; barely visible in the darkness.

"You didn't drive in, after her?" Sylvia asked.

"I didn't want my truck getting stuck in there. How would I explain that to my dad?"

Cautiously, they turned to the opening, and continued driving on. The road was rough. Overgrown with weeds, littered with fallen branches and roots, emerging from the ground. Even though it was dark, the car's headlights did verify one thing, Andie's car had been through here recently. At least someone's car had. The tire ruts left behind were fresh in the moist, impressionable ground.

"There's light up ahead."

Sylvia was pointing to the curtain of moonlight that hung about a quarter mile ahead of them. Max tried not to push the *Volvo* too much as it obediently climbed across the unforgiving terrain, premium insurance or not. But he was too damn excited. Excited about what, he wasn't sure. He didn't expect to find Andie beyond this clearing in the forest, in fact part of him hoped he wouldn't; because that would mean…it would mean she was…*well, wouldn't it?*

As the car escaped the tree cover, and emerged triumphantly into the open meadow, the brilliant moonlight lifted all of their spirits; at least a little. Except, where was the house? There was nothing here, the ground was devoid of anything, except a soft blanket of grass. Max slammed on the brakes once more.

"Where's the fuckin' house?" Max demanded.

Both of them looked inquisitively back at Jordan. The boy's eyes were riddled with fear.

"Uh, yeah, that's what I meant about not thinking I'm crazy."

"What do you mean?" Sylvia's tone was sincere and reassuring.

She'd decided, since they seemed to be playing good cop/bad cop, she'd take the role of the former; the timid kid seemed to respond to gentle coaxing, rather than prodding; something she'd done just a few hours earlier with the email accusation. Something she was feeling guilty about now, looking at the pain in Jordan's eyes.

"When we went inside, I saw things…" his voice trailed off.

"What kind of things, Jordan?" Max's tone was surprisingly soft and laced with concern this time.

Jordan looked up at them.

"Terrifying things. I—I—couldn't stay in that house another minute longer. I called for Tommy, told him we had to go. I bolted for that front door and I didn't stop running.

THE HAND THAT FEEDS YOU

Not until I'd reached the edge of the woods. Then I turned around, expecting to see Tommy running behind me...but... he never made it out of that house."

He covered his face with his hands.

Sylvia reached out and gently touched his hand.

"How do you know? Maybe you just didn't see him—"

"The house fuckin' disappeared!" Jordan's eyes were more resolute than ever.

He lost Sylvia with this, I mean, did this kid honestly expect them to believe—

"It's OK, Jordan. We believe you," Max said tenderly.

Sylvia did a double-take.

"We...do?" she asked.

"Come on, let's get out and look around. Jordan, you can stay in here, OK?"

Bewildered, Sylvia followed Max outside of the car. He decided to take the keys, just in case Jordan got any bright ideas; but the kid deserved a break. He'd done his job.

"Um, what was that? You go from thinking the kid's a total liar, to believing some bullshit story about a disappearing house? Or is this all part of some plan?"

She demanded to know what he was up to.

"Jordan's telling the truth."

"What? What are you talking about? About the house —"

"Disappearing? *Yes*, that's *exactly* what I'm talking about."

"How do you know?"

This time her tone was the one that was accusatory.

"Because Pete said the same exact thing!"

Both of them went silent.

Totally silent.

This was a lot for both of them to take in.

A self-proclaimed skeptic and a full-blown, mantra spouting, astrology-loving, glorified witch doctor, the oddest of odd couples, both being challenged on what they believed and what they could accept. In that moment, the two were one.

"So, what now?" she asked.

Max surveyed the landscape. No house, that was obvious. But it was so dark out here, even under the voluptuous moon; maybe there was something out here, something they were missing.

Wait a minute!

There was something, a dark shape watched them

from a distance, closer to the coast.

"Come on...keep quiet," Max whispered as they both crept closer and closer.

It was...a car!

"Oh my god!" the pair exclaimed in unison.

They ran as fast as they could to get a closer look.

"It's Andie's car!" Max couldn't believe it.

But, if it's here, where's she?

Aside from the car, there was nothing. No signs of a struggle, no litter scattered about; of course the strong winds from the sea would've swept any light debris away with it. Neither Max, nor Sylvia were sure just what they were looking for, but they were certain that if any incriminating evidence existed, they'd surely find it. Inside, the car was clean. It wasn't locked, so, after a preliminary glance in the front and backseats, Max pulled the trunk release. Both of them slowly walked to the back of the car, afraid to glance in the open trunk, afraid of what they might see.

Pfew.

Both breathed an audible sigh of relief.

The trunk was empty.

Well, there was a purse and a tote bag, but no dead bodies.

"You search back here. I'm gonna search the car," Max insisted.

The floorboards were clean. No signs of blood or anything out of the ordinary. Same with the seats. The center armrest had some ink pens and loose change. That just left the glove compartment; whose contents were just as unrewarding. A half-chewed pack of gum, a phone charger, a magazine, and a handful of napkins. Except, *wait a minute*. This napkin had something written on it.

Max placed the napkin on the passenger seat and shined his phone's flashlight on it. There, scribbled in pen, was a strange poem:

> Shrouded in darkness
> She lies in wait
> Luring foolish men
> To tempt their fate
> For her coffers filled
> With treasures untold
> But hasten their escape

THE HAND THAT FEEDS YOU

Lest their souls she should hold.

What the...? Max wondered what it meant?

This was Andie's handwriting. He knew it with one look. But, she didn't write poetry. This wasn't her writing style anyway. Maybe more of the napkins had writing on them. He grabbed the next one, placed it on the seat, and discovered the same thing was written on it. Then another, only, this one had it written twice, then one had it written three times…with each one the pen had dug itself deeper and deeper into the delicate surface of the paper.

One by one, he pulled a napkin out to inspect it, each bore the same bizarre script; each written more times than the last, each written more desperately, more feverishly.

What the actual fuck?

Was Andie losing it? These weren't the writings of a sane person, were they? No, they couldn't be. The last napkin sealed the deal. It was written by a fucking lunatic. Some real, *Beautiful Mind* shit. Every inch of the napkin was used to record the words, in varied degrees of font, the scale of the letters, the degree to which they'd been scrawled…all of it told the story. Something was possessing Andie, if it was indeed Andie who'd written this. He tried to convince himself that maybe he was wrong about the handwriting. But he knew better. *It was Andie's.*

"I found something!" Sylvia's voice rang out from the trunk.

A welcomed interruption to tear Max away from the prospects that were running through his mind. He wadded the napkins, and put them in his pocket. *More secrets. Just like the dreams.*

"What is it?" he asked, appearing from the side of the car.

"Eleanor Bond wants to pretend that she's never met up with Andie, huh? Then let's see her explain this!" Sylvia practically squealed, holding up Eleanor's business card.

Turns out, there was a very good reason that Andie had Eleanor's business card in her purse. Eleanor had given it to her.

*****

That last morning Andie had spent at the Taylors', after breakfast, after meeting Jordan outside at her car, Andie crawled into the driver's seat and planned her next move. *Eleanor Bond, huh? Let's see what we can find about you online.* A quick web search told Andie all she needed to know. Eleanor was a busy woman, a very busy woman. The top search results contained links to all of her social media accounts.

There were photos of her at ribbon cutting ceremonies, fundraising events, and multiple photos of her standing next to a yard sign, which read "garden of the year" an honor that she seemed to win year after year. The article attached mentioned *Magnolia Street*, no address, but it was a start. From there, Andie opened the maps app on her phone, and searched for *Magnolia Street*, set the mode to street view, a few swipes up and *holy shit*! There it was, the house from the photo. *300 Magnolia Street*, according to the app. She put the address in her phone, and started the navigation. For a moment, she didn't know whether she should be impressed at her super sleuth skills, or repulsed by how easy it was to stalk someone online.

As the car rounded onto Magnolia, Andie marveled at the stunning scene. It looked like a postcard, or a painting. Almost too perfect to be real. Beneath the warm, amber glow of the street lamps, perched high on their wrought iron posts, a fresh, wet blanket of fallen leaves seemed to flicker like delicate flames, atop the brick-pavement. Picturesque houses lined either side of the street.

There it is.

She spotted the house immediately. With its scale and its soft pools of glowing light, it begged to be noticed. There was a car pulling out of the driveway, while someone stood outside the front door, watching its departure. After the car was safely out of sight, Andie slowly pulled up to the front curb and rolled down her car window. Noticing this, the figure cautiously emerged from the front door and closed in on Andie's car. It was a woman, with silvery hair, cut short into a chic style, despite being displaced from having recently rolled out of bed. She was wearing a silk, designer robe.

"Can I help you?" the woman asked.

"I'm sorry, I know it's early, but I'm looking for someone. My name is—"

"Andie Sterling?!"

"You know who I am?" Andie was surprised.

"I'm a fan! A big fan," the woman flashed a warm smile.

"I think you're probably my only fan in this town," she laughed.

"I'm Eleanor Bond, *Nora*."

You're kidding. What luck?

"Nora, you're actually the one I'm looking for. I was

wondering if I could speak with you. It's very important. I know it's early, but—"

"Actually," the woman looked around, "my husband just left, so, now's a perfect time. Why don't you pull your car around back, and I'll meet you at the back door?"

Apparently she doesn't want to be seen talking to me either, just like everyone in this town.

But, Andie did as she was told, at least the woman was willing to talk to her. That was a first.

When Andie reached the motor court around the back of the house, the backdoor was standing open. Nora stood in the doorway to the kitchen, which was blazing with light, against the dark hour of the early morning.

"Please, come in," her host beckoned.

Once inside, Nora continued,

"Have a seat."

She gestured to the island, and went on.

"I was just making some tea. Would you care for some?"

"That sounds wonderful. Thank you," Andie said, taking her seat.

A stack of Andie's novels were waiting, next to a black marker. She looked at Nora and smiled.

"I'm guessing you'd like an autograph."

"If it's no trouble," the woman blushed.

"No trouble at all," Andie said, signing the inside cover of the first book.

She signed two more, then held up the fourth.

"*The Face in the Mountain*? Not one of my better works. You really must be a fan," she laughed.

"I disagree, I love that one. It just hasn't found its audience, yet. But it will. It's a sleeper-hit, I have a sixth sense about these things."

"I like your optimism," Andie said, signing the last book.

Then, Andie noticed a heavily used notebook sitting on the far end of the island, along with it were half a dozen pens and highlighters.

"What's that?"

"Oh, that," said Nora, "I'm a bit of a writer myself. *Nothing* like your work, of course, but I do write a column for the *Hollingshead Gazette*."

Nora sat down a cup of hot tea in front of Andie, and took up position across the island, holding her own cup in both hands, then continued.

"But, I'm guessing you didn't come here to sign my

books, or hear me talk about my work, did you?"

"You can probably guess why I'm here," Andie said.

"I have a pretty good idea," Nora replied.

Andie pulled out her phone, and opened her email app.

"I received this email. Do you know anything about it?"

She handed the phone across the island. Nora's face went white.

"You didn't send it?" Andie asked.

"No, I'm sorry, I'm afraid I don't know anything about it."

Fan or not, she wasn't about to get off that easy. Her face couldn't hide the truth. She may not have sent the email, but she clearly knew a thing or two about what it referenced. Andie took the phone back, then opened the attachment.

"Then maybe you can tell me what *this* is?"

"Oh my god! I've never seen a photo of it…I mean…I didn't even know there was one—" Nora stopped herself from finishing the thought.

"So it does exist," Andie called her bluff.

"Please, Andie, I can't. I've said too much already."

"Nora, please. No one in this town will even speak

with me. You've taken me into your home. Offered me tea. That has to mean something."

Andie looked at her, pleadingly.

Nora looked empathetic for a second, then her countenance shifted and the walls went up.

"I'm a fan. That's all. Please, Miss Sterling, I just asked you in because I wanted to have you sign a few books. Maybe ask you about them. That's all."

Andie wasn't buying it. That infamous bullshit meter of hers told her that Nora wanted to be honest with her. This was all a front. She reached across the island and took Nora by the hand.

"Nora, please, as a fan, as a…friend, as a…*woman*, be honest with me. I know that you know something. Probably more than anyone else in this town. I also know, you want to tell me…so, I'm asking you, please…"

Nora's gaze rose to meet Andie's.

Andie continued.

"Tell me."

CHAPTER 20

Max and Sylvia dropped Jordan off at his truck, in front of the coffee shop. Both thanked him for all he'd told them. They also promised him that, so long as nothing came up that suggested he was tied to Andie or Tommy's disappearances, they'd keep everything he told them in strict confidence. Before he got out of the car, Max stopped him.

"One last question, Jordan."

"What?"

"Why did you send Andie that email? I get that there have been disappearances, but what did you mean about a million secrets?"

Jordan thought for a moment, choosing his words carefully.

"Obviously, you both have seen that there's more to this town than meets the eye."

He looked directly at them, then continued.

"My dad, he's told me stories. The things that have happened, the things they've tried to hide." He paused. "My mom's fine keeping them hidden. My dad won't talk much about it, but I know it really bothers him. Me?" his gaze was piercing, "I refuse to let another generation go by, sweeping it all under the rug. I can't just live with it. I *won't*."

He got out of the car, before Max could get him to clarify.

OK?

The town has secrets.

But, what the fuck is he talking about?

"What do you think he means by all of that?" Sylvia asked.

Max didn't answer, he just silently watched Jordan climb into his truck, and drive away. Wondering all the while, if he'd ever unlock the full mystery that was Hollingshead.

✹✹✹✹✹

About an hour later they were back in their hotel room. Sylvia was already sound asleep, but Max, he was restless. He wondered how she could sleep with all that had happened that night. Then he remembered, he had a bit more information than she did. The napkins, with the strange poem, were still wadded in his pocket. Once more, he felt guilty for not telling Sylvia about them, but if he could disprove the thoughts running through his mind, there'd be no need for her to share the same worries that he had.

Carefully, quietly, he dressed, grabbed his phone and keys, slipped out into the hallway, and silently closed the door behind him. He unlocked his phone, and dialed.

"Hi. Sorry, I know it's really late; I wouldn't call if it wasn't an emergency. No, I'm fine. But, I have to talk to someone, and I was wondering if we could meet up. Yeah, tonight. OK, I'm sending you the location. Did you get it? Great, can you meet me there in an hour? Thank you. I'll see you in a bit."

He hung up the phone, placed his ear to the door to make sure he could still hear Sylvia's faint snore within. Sure enough, she was out cold.

✱✱✱✱✱

It was colder now. Probably twenty to thirty degrees cooler than it had been a few hours ago. The wind had also picked up, a lot. Maybe that was part of it. The sound lapped at his ears, as if it were speaking to him. Strong gusts were thrown upward by the crashing of the waves below; bouncing off of everything in their path. The grass retched and writhed to and fro.

The meadow was even more dreadful, more uncomforting when he was alone. He hated the thought of Andie being stranded out here. *Was she still out here, somewhere? Hiding?* Max told himself that it was a stupid notion. Why would she do something like that? It didn't make sense. But, then again, neither did the napkins. That poem. He knew it wasn't her words, but he'd still heard them before. Somewhere. But, where?

"Andie!"

He drew in an even deeper breath.

"ANDIE!!!"

Even at full volume, yelling to the point of forming nodules on his vocal cords, his voice was no match for the angry sea that beckoned to him.

Maybe it had beckoned to Andie, too.

He cursed the thought, but it had been floating around the back of his mind for some time now.

"Andie, goddamn it, where are you?" he cried, silently.

The familiar roar of an engine swelled in the distance.

THE HAND THAT FEEDS YOU

Max turned to look at the forest, just as the soft glow of headlights came spilling out of the clearing where the old road had once been. He gained his composure. Promised himself that he would be rational; practical. These were qualities he'd always taken pride in being able to maintain, even when the stakes were ungodly high. He knew he had to do this, no matter how uncomfortable. This was for Andie. The woman he loved, more than life itself.

A late model *Jeep* sliced its way into the meadow, and when Max flashed the lights of his *Volvo*, it made its way over to meet him. The *Jeep* parked next to him, and the driver's door opened, a pair of dark, leather riding boots stepped out.

"I can't thank you enough for coming. Seriously, you have no idea," said Max.

"You weren't kidding about that road. It's no joke."

"Dr. Sharma—"

"Manasvi, please. We're not at the hospital," she said with a smile.

"Manasvi, I called you because, I have a friend...and *she's*...she's missing."

"Is it the woman from your phone?"

Max drew in a deep breath, then let it out.

"Is it that obvious?"

"It's obvious that it's someone you care a lot about. You wouldn't go through all of this trouble, otherwise."

"Yeah, well, she came to this town several weeks ago. No one seems to have seen or heard from her in the last week."

"Have you notified the police?"

"Yeah, about that, it's complicated. I think I'm better off to try and come at this without their help."

"I see," she sounded uncertain, "do you have any leads?"

"That's why I've asked you to come here tonight. See, at first I was thinking someone must've done something."

"You mean someone may have hurt her?"

"I thought so, she hadn't exactly been welcomed into this town with open arms. But, the more clues I get, the more I'm able to question anyone who might've had something to do with her disappearance, the more I'm not so sure anyone else is involved."

His voice went quiet as he realized what he was saying.

This was something he'd been holding at bay, in the back of his mind, but as long as he didn't come right out and say it, it wasn't a possibility, *but now?*

"That day in the hospital, you'd said something that stuck with me," Max continued.

"What's that?"

"About how people respond differently to trauma. My father died a few months ago, and it was very unexpected."

"I'm very sorry to hear that."

"Thank you. The point is, I took it hard for a few days, then went right back on living. My mother, on the other hand, she's been unable to move on. Even going so far as to spend a small fortune on psychics, or anything that can promise her a chance at communicating with him. As if he's still here, with her."

Manasvi nodded.

"Well there you go, two different people share the same experience, but grieve in very different ways."

"Exactly. Pete goes through, whatever it was that he went through, and he completely shuts down."

"And your friend?"

"When we last spoke, the night that she disappeared, she opened up to me. She told me about some very traumatic experiences in her childhood. Things that she'd never been able to let go of. And, just like you said about Pete, relieving those experiences as he talked to me about them, I'm starting to wonder if maybe…maybe Andie did the same thing when she had opened up to me."

"What makes you so sure?"

"This is her car."

He gestured to the third car next to them, then continued.

"After she and I talked, she drove straight up here, in the dead of night, and was never heard from again."

"…I see. Did she leave a note, or anything that would lead you to—"

"Actually, she did."

Max pulled out the first napkin. The doctor read the words of the poem.

"Shrouded in darkness, she lies in wait…isn't that what Pete said to you?"

Oh my god! That's where I'd heard it before! Max quietly realized.

"Exactly," Max said. "Then there's this."

Max laid down the second napkin, then the third, and so on. Each in rapid succession of the former, each showing a more and more frantic display than its predecessor.

"In your expert opinion," Max began, "do these seem

like the writings of a crazy person?" His voice was a little more desperate than he wanted it to be.

"Max, I can understand your concern—"

"Please, I have to know. Am I just wasting my time here? Doesn't it make more sense that she's just...laying beneath the waves down there?!"

He pointed to the sea below them. His composure was all gone now, so much for that plan.

"Max, listen to me," her voice told him to get a hold of himself, "I know what this looks like. And, it's easy to draw conclusions."

He nodded.

"But," she continued, "we don't have all the facts here. We're trying to draw a conclusion that supports the evidence we have, rather than trying to disprove our theory until it can no longer hold up. That's the exact opposite of the scientific method. And when emotions are involved, it's even easier for things to become clouded. Our judgment's compromised."

He sighed, she was right. He'd been too emotional to think rationally, even when he thought he had been.

"Let me give you a hypothetical," said Manasvi, "let's say that you decided that you *were* just wasting your time here. You pack your things, go home, and move on with your life. Six months from now, a year from now, how do you feel? Are you still thinking about her, or were you able to move on? Do you feel like you made the right choice?"

"No. Of course not, it'd continue to eat away at me. I don't know that I would ever fully move on from it," he said with certainty.

"Well then, there's your answer."

She looked directly into his eyes.

"Max, until you find out what happened, whatever it may have been, until you get that closure, I don't think you should stop looking."

He breathed a deep breath of relief.

She was right.

Of course she was right. What was he thinking?

A moment of weakness, that's all it was. He was allowed to have that, wasn't he? After all, he *was* human. No matter where Andie was, dead or alive, no matter what may or may not have happened to her…no matter how long it may take, he was going to find out.

CHAPTER 21

"You two are becoming some of my best customers," Bennett was grinning from ear to ear.

"Best damn cup of coffee in town!" Max laughed, holding up his cup.

"I don't know about the coffee, never touch the stuff, but your rosemary mint tea is simply divine," Sylvia chimed in.

"That's what I love to hear."

Bennett added a playful wink for good measure. Then he remembered something.

"Oh, by the way, since you two have become regulars,

I figured I'd just go ahead and bring this in with me and give it to you this morning."

He placed a duffle bag on the table between them.

"It's Andie's," he went on, "I was able to fit everything she left in it. But I haven't looked through anything, scout's honor."

He threw up a hand.

"Thanks. You might just be the only decent person in this entire town," Max said with a shrug.

"Any news? Anything since yesterday?" Bennett asked.

"We've got one lead to follow-up on. Hopefully that'll give us something, otherwise, I think we're pretty much *S.O.L.*"

"Bennett," Sylvia said, "I know you can't talk about the town's history, *per se*; but could you tell us something about the disappearances that happened around these parts? Surely you must know something."

She gave her best pair of puppy dog eyes.

"Uh, nothing much, I'm afraid. Only ones I know about happened years ago. Probably no truth to 'em, anyway, ya know?"

Even Bennett, kind as he was, didn't seem to be

willing to touch on the all-too-sacred mysteries surrounding Hollingshead.

"I tell you what, though, if I think of anything, I'll tell you. *OK*? And if there's anything else I can do, please, don't hesitate."

"Thank you," said Max.

Sylvia just nodded, politely.

"I'll get to work on your drinks," Bennett double-tapped his pen on his ticket book, then waltzed away.

The two that remained looked at the black duffle bag that sat, wedged between them.

"Shall we?" Sylvia asked.

"After you," Max made a sweeping gesture.

Sylvia drew back the zipper and rummaged inside. The contents consisted mostly of clothes, a pair, make that two pairs of shoes, and, "what's this?" Sylvia's hand withdrew a small, leather-bound book.

"Andie's journal," Max murmured.

He knew that book, it had sat across from him in numerous book pitch sessions. She took it with her everywhere. She slept with it right next to her. Anytime inspiration came, maybe a thought for a story, character description or motive, even just a fanciful flow of dialogue that she liked, Andie would write it all down. At least that's all he'd ever seen her use it for.

What if she used it for other things?

Personal thoughts?

Reprieve?

Max knew that there was a chance that, reading the journal, they may discover the kinds of thoughts that really went through Andie's head. Maybe she wrote about her true feelings for Max. Was he ready for that? What if she wrote that she didn't really feel the way about him that he hoped she did?

What if it was more of the strange, unbridled chaos of incoherent consciousness…like he'd seen on those napkins.

"Sylvia?" he decided it was time.

Sylvia did deserve to know.

About *the napkins*.

About *dreams*.

After all, holding on to all of this information wasn't fair. Deliberately withholding it meant that he was just as selfish and petty as he'd often been told by others. By his logic, all of his naysayers simply didn't understand. There was a method to his madness. He wasn't trying to be stingy. To be a know-it-all. Except, he was. Suddenly, it was all clear to him now.

"There's something I need to show you."

He placed the napkins on the table and the two of them discussed the findings. Max apologized for keeping them a secret, citing that he wanted to protect their image of Andie; something he now realized could be open for discussion.

"Max, I already knew," she replied, after he'd finished telling her about Andie's unpleasant childhood.

"You knew?"

"Of course, I told you that we'd discussed things that she hadn't told anyone else."

"So, what do you make of this?"

"It's hard to say…but she wasn't crazy, Max. She wasn't depressed, I mean, no more than you or I."

"Then what do you make of the napkins? Surely she must've been going through *something*."

"Maybe we'll find out more in her journal," Sylvia said, cracking open the book's cover.

"Wait a minute!" Max realized he hadn't told her about his dreams yet.

"What is it?" she asked, looking up at him.

"Um…what's it say?" he asked.

Instead of bringing up his dreams, instead of engaging in another lengthy conversation, he was ready to know what that journal said.

Who was Andie?

The *real* Andie?

Sylvia began reading the page, aloud:

"The room was round. There was a flagstone floor and field-stone walls—"

"Waitaminute!"

He cut her off.

"Sylvia, let me see that."

She handed the book to him and he picked up reading where she left off.

"Floating timbered beams stretched across the lonely expanse overhead. A fire roared within the carved stone fireplace-that took up nearly the entire wall against which it sat."

He closed the book and looked up at her, a lost expression on his face.

"What is it?" she asked.

"It's my dream."

"What dream? Andie wrote about your dream?"

"But she couldn't have," Max thought aloud, "how

could she know?"

Max opened back up the book and skimmed through the pages. Sure enough, every one of his dreams had been written down in that journal.

"Are you gonna tell me what's going on, or not?" Sylvia cocked an eyebrow.

Max took a deep breath, then began to explain everything to her. He told her about each dream, the girl, the burning house, the angry mob who came to dispose of the woman…oh…only *after* the crazy woman had performed the strange magic trick with the fire.

"So, you're saying she made the house disappear? This, mysterious woman?"

Max sat back in his chair, putting the pieces together.

"I guess I am," he said.

He couldn't believe it himself.

"So, you're saying that you saw visions of things that *actually* happened? Things that must be what makes up the dark history of this town, the things that no one will talk about. And, somehow, Andie has them all written down in her journal?"

"I know it sounds crazy…" Max said.

"You're right, it does." Sylvia said, scratching her

chin.

"There has to be some rational—"

"Crazy, but not impossible," she cut him off.

"Huh?" Max asked, bewildered.

Sylvia's countenance shifted. Her expression was definitive. It was certain.

She leaned in.

"Andie is speaking to you, through your dreams."

Max laughed at this, until he realized Sylvia wasn't laughing.

"Wait. You're serious?"

"Dreams are a powerful thing. Very powerful. We're taught to disregard them, as just our subconscious having free rein when we're too weak to control it. But, dreams can be used to move between realms. To show us things that have happened or that will happen. Or…to communicate with those who have crossed over."

Max's face fell.

"What do you mean cross over?" he asked.

Silence.

"You think she's—"

"I think some part of her is still here. And it wants to communicate with you…in the only way she knows how. As a little girl, she learned how to control her dreams, to manipulate them. I think, now, she's held onto that ability, to reach out to you."

"I don't know," Max sighed, skeptically.

"And we won't know…unless we try. You've got to try, Max. Do it…for Andie."

The woman's eyes were pleading.

He softened up just looking at them.

He'd *definitely* developed a soft spot for her.

And, she was right, after all he had witnessed of late, the more and more he opened up his mind to the possibilities of things unseen, who's to say Andie wasn't talking to him through dreams? After all, how else could he explain the connection between his dreams and Andie's journal? Even though it wouldn't be pleasant, I mean those dreams were fucking terrible, it was worth a shot. Probably the best shot they had at this moment.

"OK, I'll do it. For Andie," he relented.

Sylvia's face lit up.

"Good. Maybe you aren't such a pile of shit after all," she laughed.

"I wouldn't go that far," he said.

CHAPTER 22

"You stay right where you are," the assistant said, picking up the phone, then began speaking into the receiver.

"Security!"

"Excuse me, please, I think there's been a mistake," Max leaned on the desk, playfully, flashing that dashing smile.

Sylvia wasn't the only one who knew how to work a little magic.

"Sorry, I don't think I caught your name," he continued, dialing up the charm even further.

"Maven," the assistant said with a blush.

Max's bullshit was working.

"Ah, Maven, that's a beautiful name."

He took the receiver from her hand, without her realizing it and hung it up. He went on.

"You see, Eleanor and I had an appointment scheduled today, and she told me to just swing by her office this morning."

"Well, she doesn't have it marked on her schedule."

"It'll just take a minute," he said with a wink.

"Right now she's on a phone call," the assistant looked past him at Sylvia, "and I've been given strict orders not to allow that woman anywhere near that office."

She nodded towards a heavy pair of sleek, dark doors.

"You mean *this* office?" Sylvia asked, making mad a dash for the doors.

"Get away from there! Security! Secur—" her words were cut short as the woman burst into Eleanor's office.

Max trailed behind them. Like the exterior of the building and the reception room within, the office was tasteful and upscale. Tan grasscloth wallpaper, thick baseboard trim and crown molding anchored the hand-scraped wood floors and the coffered ceilings respectively.

There were linen upholstered chairs and a tufted sofa, oversized table lamps, and a hand-knotted Persian rug brought some muted color into the room.

Nora sat behind a desk of glass and polished chrome, talking on the phone. When she saw the three intruders sweep into her office, she simply said,

"Amaury, I'm going to have to call you back."

Then she hung up the phone. She didn't yell. She didn't jump up from her desk. She didn't respond in a way that any of them had assumed she might.

"Ma'am, I'm so sorry, I tried to stop her—"

"That's quite alright," Nora stood up and walked around to greet her guests.

"Please, have a seat, both of you."

Everyone seemed terribly confused, except for Nora, she knew *exactly* what she was doing.

Max and Sylvia moved into the office and each took one of the linen chairs that faced the desk.

"Ma'am, if you'd like me to call security—"

"That won't be necessary, Maven. We're fine. Thank you," said the mayor's wife, in a tone that had just the slightest touch of condescension.

"Ma'am," the assistant whispered again.

"We're fine, Maven. Thank you!" Sylvia said, leaning out of her chair to make her point; except her tone *was* dripping with condescension. Loads of it.

"That'll be all," Nora insisted.

Before the assistant could say another word, the impressive pair of doors were closed right in the woman's face, trapping her outside of the office.

"You'll have to excuse her. I'd fire her, if she weren't so damn good at her job...*that* and, well, if she weren't my *niece*," Nora laughed.

Then, she casually strolled around the two of them. Rather than opting for the chair behind her desk, she perched herself on the corner of her desk, mere feet from the pair of intruders. She crossed her wrists and gently folded them onto her lap, her gold bangles clicking as they met each other. She smiled, then said,

"My, my. You two certainly have a flair for *theatrics*, don't you."

Was she being serious right now?

This was the same woman who released the hounds on Sylvia, for simply mentioning Andie's name, not even twenty four hours ago. Making threats against them, if they were to ever come near her again. Now, here she was, inviting them into her office, unannounced. Making jokes with them. Had she experienced some change of heart? Or was she up to something?

Sylvia looked at Max and gave him a quick nod. Max retrieved Nora's business card from his wallet and held it up.

"Do you recognize this?" he demanded.

"Of course, it's my card," she smiled.

"Do you know where we got it?" Sylvia chimed in.

"We found it in Andie's purse!" Max blurted out, before Nora had the chance to say anything.

"Are you still gonna pretend like you and Andie never spoke to each other?" he snapped.

"No, of course not," Nora smiled yet again.

"No! You won't—wait. You *don't* deny it?" he asked, confused.

"Not at all. Andie and I spoke a great deal. At least we spoke for a while. It was just the *once*."

"Wait, wait, wait," Sylvia threw a hand up, "then *why* did you lie about it?"

"I didn't lie."

Nora's tone was incredulous, almost pious. Sylvia was furious.

"I specifically asked you if you'd met with Andie—"

"OK, *first of all*, you practically accosted me, in front of my husband no less, and as you both know he isn't exactly Andie's biggest fan. And, *secondly*, I didn't meet with Andie, *OK*? She met with me."

"A technicality," Sylvia groaned, throwing her head back in disgust.

"My dear, one does not successfully navigate a demanding career and nearly forty years of marriage, without understanding and appreciating the power of getting off on a technicality. It's saved my marriage more than once," Nora laughed.

"OK, so you and Andie spoke! Can we all just agree on *that*?" Max wasn't in the mood for games.

"Yes, fine. We spoke."

"OK, what did you talk about?" Max asked.

Nora's face dropped. The lighthearted smile was gone. A look of worry had taken its place. She stood up and began pacing the room. Something she routinely did when she became nervous.

After a few moments, she stopped, and with her back to them,

"Look, I know what you must think of me."

Oh, you don't wanna know, Sylvia thought.

"Truth is," Nora went on, "if you hadn't come to find me, then I was going to come find you."

She turned to face them.

"Why?" asked Max.

"It was something Andie said to me, she, really got me thinking about things..."

"What kind of things?" Sylvia asked.

Nora hesitated for a moment, then finally took the path that led behind her desk, took her chair, and reached into her purse.

"Do either of you have your phone on you?" Nora asked, pulling out her own.

Both Max and Sylvia reached for their phones at the same time.

"Yes, of course you do," Nora continued, "it wouldn't be the twenty-first century if everyone didn't have their cellphones on them at all times. Do either of you have your *Bluetooth* on?"

Before Max could speak, Nora said,

"*Max's Phone*? So typical," she laughed. "There, I just sent you something. Did you accept it?"

"Not yet–"

"Well hurry up, Max. Before I change my mind."

"What's she doing?" Sylvia asked.

"She's dropping me a file," Max said.

"You mean, like email?"

"No, with *Bluetooth*. I just got it," he said.

"You can do that?" Sylvia asked, looking at Max, then at Nora.

"Not bad for an old lady, huh?" Nora joked.

"What is it?" asked Max.

"It's an audio file of our conversation. Mine and Andie's."

Max went to press *play*, then,

"Don't play it!" Nora said.

Max stopped. She continued.

"Not now, not...*here*. You have to promise me that you won't play that anywhere that someone might hear it. Got it?" Nora implored.

Max and Sylvia shook their heads.

"Promise me!" Nora was serious.

"I promise," their replies came in unison.

"Everything you need to know, everything you've been searching for...you'll find it in there. Maybe, after hearing it, you'll be able to plan your next move. And... maybe...I'll be able to figure out *mine*."

A look of hope made its way into her face. She almost smiled at them; *almost*.

"But I'll tell you the same thing I told Andie."

"What's that?" Max asked.

"Stay skeptical. Trust no one. Trust nothing," her face turned very serious. "Got it?"

Max and Sylvia nodded, silently.

"Good."

Nora's countenance did a one-eighty, and she gave them an annoyed, or *maybe* it was a playful glance.

"Alright, now get out of here, so I can get back to work. Maven!"

The doors burst open so fast that the woman must've been listening up against the other side of them the entire time.

"Ma'am?" asked the assistant.

"Please see Ms. Gold and Mr. Tate out of my office."

"With pleasure," the condescension belonged wholly to Maven now.

"Oh, and one last thing," Nora crossed to meet them in the doorway, "I trust this is the last time our paths will cross. In fact, if you ever approach my husband or I while we're out in public, or if you set foot in this office again…

well…don't make me finish that thought."

"But what if we—" Max began.

"That'll be all," Nora cut him off.

And with that, she slammed the double-doors in *their faces* this time.

Message sent. Message received.

Safely back inside the *Volvo*, Max connected this phone's *Bluetooth* to the car stereo.

"What do you think is on it?" Sylvia asked.

"Only one way to find out," he said.

Then, he pressed *play*.

CHAPTER 23

"It's Wednesday, September 28th," Andie's voice was the first one on the recording, "and I'm sitting in the kitchen of Eleanor Bond. Eleanor, do I have your permission to record?"

There was a pause, then Andie said,

"Nora I'm going to need you to verbalize it."

"Yes, I consent to being recorded," Nora said.

"Thank you, Nora, I really appreciate you taking the time to speak with me about this. So, I guess, just start from the beginning. When did this all start?"

"In the mid-eighteen hundreds, a man by the name of Carlisle Cartwright lived in this town. He was a self-proclaimed inventor, but if you ask me he was more of a swindler than anything. None of his inventions ever amounted to anything, and after a while he'd gotten enough of a bad reputation with investors, that he decided to try his prospects elsewhere. So he moved to Europe. Now the details are fuzzy about what all happened in Europe, but eventually he moved to Romania and began courting the daughter of a wealthy Romanian business owner. Belinda was a socialite, and both she and her father were taken with Western culture and were taken by this handsome, American inventor. When Carlisle asked for Belinda's hand, her father said that if Carlisle could produce just one invention that was successful, then not only could he marry her, but he'd be made a very wealthy man. And you know what happened?"

"What?" Andie asked.

"The sonofabitch did it!"

Nora laughed.

"He *actually* did it. Developed some electric-type boiler that was used to create steam for Turkish Baths. These types of baths were very popular in the elite social clubs at the time. So, the two were married, and Carlisle became a millionaire.

Everything seemed perfect, for a while, until Belinda realized that she couldn't have children. You have to understand, this was a time when women were expected to bear children. If they couldn't, then it was assumed that there must be something wrong with them. Carlisle was still an American citizen, so adoption wasn't really a viable option for them. So, they devised a plan. They hired a poor, Romanian woman to carry a child for them.

Again, different times, right? No fertility clinics. No *In Vitro*. No turkey basters," Nora laughed, "so they had to do it the old-fashioned way."

"You mean...?"

"Yep, Carlisle did the deed with the Romanian lady. What a guy, huh? Problem solved, *right*? Wrong. Before the child was born, a revolution sprang up. *The Wallachian Revolution of 1848* saw an uprising against the aristocracy within Romania; the effects of which were still being felt some twenty years later, when Cartwright joined the ranks of Romania's elite. Carlisle and his family would surely have been targeted, had they chose to remain. So, they fled back to America. Back to Hollingshead, the town he'd once called home."

"And the Romanian woman, the one carrying the child?" Andie asked.

"Camilla! *That's right*, I knew her name would come

to me," Nora said. "They brought her with them. Carlisle, Belinda, and her father, all of them relished in their new American life. This was during the end of the Victorian Era, the Edwardian Era was fast approaching, a time that history would call *The Gilded Age*. Steel, the railroad, textiles, manufacturing, industry was booming in America and it was creating millionaires faster than you can imagine. These folks lived a life of opulence, of privilege, the likes of which history had never seen; at least not outside of royalty. They were the new royalty. Men would roll their cigars in one hundred dollar bills, just to light them on fire and smoke them, simply because they could. Flashing their wealth, that's what these folks lived for, Carlisle and his family were no exception.

They purchased a large parcel of land along the coast, overlooking the town, even paid to lay the road leading up to the property. Camilla gave birth to the child, a girl, whom they called Isabella. They doted and spoiled the child; giving her everything she could ever want. After relinquishing her role as surrogate, Camilla fell back into position as Belinda's servant; often acting as a governess when the girl's parents traveled.

But, all was far from perfect. Carlisle, try as he might,

had a hard time fitting back in with the folks of the town. He seemed different, to them, he'd changed. It wasn't just the money. Bringing back a bride, and her father, from a foreign country, and even more so, the strange governess, a dark woman with peculiar habits; none of them were ever truly welcomed as members of the town. So, Carlisle and his family remained, almost in exile, in their lavish coastal mansion."

"So the people of this town shunned them?" Andie asked.

"I don't think they shunned them," Nora said, "I think it's safe to say that they tolerated them. Carlisle would throw lavish parties, inviting the nobility of town to join them, which they generally would, for appearances sake, if nothing else. Historically, in the ranks of high society, when someone from your circle invited you to a social engagement, you were expected to attend. To see and be seen. Declining an invitation, without a valid excuse, would be seen as vulgar. Something befitting of the lower classes. It was a good way to become the subject of gossip.

And, it was on one such occasion, a birthday party for their daughter, Bella, that the history, the future of Hollingshead would be forever changed. Dozens of families from this town, as well as those surrounding it, ventured up that narrow road to the Cartwright Mansion. Little did they know that the girl's party would also be their funeral."

"What happened?" Andie asked.

"A fire. An immense fire consumed the mansion, and for some strange reason, no one escaped. No one, that is, except for the little girl, Bella, and her birth mother, the strange, Romanian woman. Of course rumors went flying. Everyone seemed to have their own theories about what happened, but it was generally believed that the fire must've been caused by this, strange, foreign woman. A witch, by most accounts. It was the only thing that made any sense, to the locals at least. I mean, there were no survivors to corroborate their theory. When the folks went up to the party and never returned, the rumor mill began churning.

A group of townsfolk, vigilantes, armed with torches and pitchforks, something straight outta the movies, decided to take matters into their own hands. When they arrived at the site, sure enough, they found the strange woman and the little girl. Just enough to confirm their suspicions were correct. What happened next has been blown out of proportion, I'm sure. Ask ten people, you'll get ten different answers, but, basically, they decided to weigh the woman down and toss her into the sea. But, before they could, she cast a spell upon them, upon the house. She called upon a dark fog, which trapped everyone and everything in it. Unable to see, a number of the men, thirteen to be exact, fell into the sea; as did the woman. These men would become the only recorded disappearances in Hollingshead.

After the fog lifted, the house was *gone*. Legend has it that the house is still there, that the woman hid it, in plain sight, that it only appears in the fog. If one ventures inside, and the fog lifts, they'll be trapped inside until it appears again."

"And, what about the girl? What happened to her?" Andie asked.

"To be honest, I'm not sure. She was brought back to the town, placed with a foster family, but she later ran away. To my knowledge she was never seen, nor heard from again."

"Wow."

Andie took a minute to process.

"Yeah, it's a lot, I know," said Nora.

"So, how do you know so much about all of this?"

"My grandmother was about Bella's age. She and her family were supposed to attend the party, but at the last minute, my grandmother fell ill," Nora chuckled, "I suppose it's probably the only time someone's life was spared by catching a cold. Not only their life, but their entire family's as well."

"You're probably right," Andie laughed.

"So, there you have it. I suppose if someone's going to write it into a story, at least that someone's you," Nora said with a smile.

"Again," Andie began, "I really do appreciate you telling me. I guess that just leaves one question."

"What's that?" Nora asked.

"Why aren't you telling me everything?"

"What? I have told you everything—"

"Nora, we're *both* storytellers. Me with my books, you with your newspaper column. Getting to the bottom of a story, that's what we do. I know when there's more to be told. Your story, while it is grim and dark, doesn't explain why this town is so hell-bent on keeping it all a secret. That may be part of the story, but it's not the *whole story*."

The recording went silent for a second. Max could picture Nora pacing about her kitchen, trying to plan her next move. Andie had caught her. She was good at that.

"You're good," Nora said with a chuckle, "I know I shouldn't be surprised, but damn, you're good."

"So, will you tell me?" Andie asked softly.

"You don't understand, even if I wanted to…I made a promise. Long ago. I gave my word that I would never speak of it to anyone. I know people break promises all the time, but I'm not most people. When I make a vow to someone, it has to mean something. You know? Telling you, even if it feels like the right thing—"

"Nora, do you know why I'm here? Why I came to this town?"

"Because you got an email—"

"I get hundreds of emails every month. Probably a dozen or more telling me about some urban legend that they want me to explore, some idea for a story that they want me to write; many of them are more intriguing than the one I've shown you. No, I'm here because, because I trusted my gut. See, when I read that email, I felt something. My gut told me that there was a story here. Something had been covered up, years ago. And it was still being covered up. I wanted to expose it. I needed to expose it. To hold those guilty, accountable. To find justice for those who'd been victimized. I can't explain it, it's just an instinct."

Andie looked Nora in the eye.

"I know that *you* know what that feels like. I can see it

in your eyes. I saw it the moment we met. I'm here because you want to tell me. You want to get, *whatever it is*, off your chest. It's been holding you prisoner for years. Maybe all of your life. And I respect you wanting to keep your word, I do, but Nora, do me a favor. Listen to your gut. If it's telling you to keep quiet, like you have been all these years, then I'll go. I'll write a story with what you've given me." Andie leaned in even closer. "But, if your gut is telling you that it's time, time to break your silence, to set yourself free…then please… Nora, tell me the truth."

All went quiet once more. The recording still had plenty of time left, Max verified just to be sure. *Good. Andie must've gotten her to talk*, he thought.

"You're right," Nora finally said, "about everything. Well, *before I begin*, you must understand, these were different times. People were motivated by fear. Fear of what they didn't understand. Fear still motivates people to act irrationally, you know? You see it every time you turn on the news."

She was on a bit of a tangent now.

"Nora, *please*?" Andie reined her back in.

Another brief pause, and then,

"As far back as I can remember, my childhood was…

a dream," Nora reflected. "I was an only child, but my parents, grandparents, all of those around me surrounded me with so much love. My family had been in this town since its inception. Having been born into a life of wealth and privilege, I can honestly say, I wanted for nothing. The men in my family have always held some political position in the town; influencing the lives of the citizens and ensuring their livelihood. My grandfather, the apple of my eye, and I of his, was mayor back then.

"*Prosperity and Progress, Prosperity and Progress.*" I can still hear him giving those campaign speeches. He may've been right about the prosperity, this town has always succeeded, financially. It's the progressive part that made a hypocrite out of him. Out of all of us.

I suppose the first time I noticed anything, I must've been a teenager, maybe thirteen or fourteen. A group of families had moved in from New York state. They looked like us. Talked like us, but they were *different*. Or so I had been told. "*Goddamn catholics*," my father would growl at the dinner table. "*Language, John, language*," my mother would giggle. She never had any more to say on the matter. I couldn't understand what the big deal was, I was friends with some of their children. They were perfectly good people.

THE HAND THAT FEEDS YOU

Shortly after they'd built their church, a modest little building on the edge of town, the town saw its first disappearance since the fire up at the Cartwright mansion. Two men had gone missing, and it soon became rumored that the catholic families had something to do with it. Of course they didn't, but without any evidence to suggest what really happened, this became accepted as truth by most in the town. One morning, the town awoke to find that the catholic church had been burned to the ground, and all of the families had left town.

Then, a short time later, a family moved into town that *did* look different than us. The elders of the family were former slaves, who'd worked hard to buy their freedom. Later in life they'd decided to leave the South, to encourage a better life for their children; and their children's children. I thought it was a wonderful thing to watch, the sort of progress my grandfather had stumped on and on about so many times. But I soon realized that not everyone felt the same way. Many in the town took their complaints to my grandfather, and he reassured them that all would be taken care of.

But, that family didn't stick around long either. Nor did the Irish immigrants who came after them. Nor the Italians after them. I should've noticed a pattern sooner, but I was still just a teenager. Blithely believing that my family was good, just, and upright. That the words we sang about in our church hymnal, about love and the freedom that comes from knowing God, about how we're all God's creatures; I believed that it was all true. I believed that they all believed it too.

The one time I spoke to my grandfather about it, about my doubts that the folks of this town really were as open and accepting as they should be of newcomers, he just laughed and told me that I was letting my imagination run away with me. But, you mentioned that *gut feeling*. I knew, in my gut, there was more to it than that. *Much more*. I just didn't know how much. I wasn't ready for just how much more there really was.

Then, one night, after my father had gone on and on at the dinner table about the "*fuckin' sprites*," two men who were roommates, but not married, I had that sinking feeling that they'd be the next to be ran out of town. Oh, how I wish they had been.

I was awakened around midnight, by the sound of a foghorn. Have you ever heard a foghorn?" Nora asked.

"In movies, I guess," Andie chuckled. "Never in real life."

"Creepy sound. Very ominous...*terrifying* when it wakes you up from sleep."

"I'd imagine so," Andie agreed.

"We have one on the outer banks. Usually used to signal ships, when it's too foggy to see the coast. Before the days of text-alerts, the town also used it as sort of an emergency warning system. Alerting citizens to be on-watch for danger. Anytime it was signaled, citizens were warned to stay indoors. After the number of incidents I'd witnessed, I was convinced that this must be another disappearance. But I was through sitting idly-by, with no answers. My curiosity wouldn't allow me to go back to sleep. I *had* to know what was going on.

I tiptoed out of my room, and listened from the top of the stairs. My father and grandfather stood in the foyer talking to my mother; as they were getting ready to head outside. "*It's time,*" they told my mother. "*Be careful. Both of you,*" she said, giving my father a kiss. Then she helped both men into their long, hooded robes. I'd never seen these before. They were a heavy, velvet fabric, in a deep blood red color. They drew their hoods up, concealing their faces, each grabbed a lantern, then ventured out into the cold, dark veil of night.

I waited for my mother to leave the foyer, then quietly made my own way outside. I had to know where they were going. What they were doing. From a safe distance I followed the men. At least ten to fifteen paces behind, without making a sound. I couldn't hear what they were talking about, since it was no more than a whisper and with their back to me. If I could just get a little bit closer. They rounded a corner and then, I lost them."

"They disappeared?" Andie asked, confused.

"No, I lost them in a sea of others. People from the town. Probably a hundred of them. All wearing the same, red robe, the same hood drawn up to cast their face in shadows; protecting their identity. They glowed like ghostly, crimson orbs, in the foggy darkness. One man, whose voice I couldn't instantly recognize, took charge in the center of the group. "*It is time, my brothers and sisters. Time to cleanse this town of the evil that threatens it.*"

With that, the man raised his lantern, and each in the crowd responded with the like. Then, moving as one, in perfect procession, without a sound, they moved like a ghost through the streets of the town; until they came to the home where the *sprites* lived. With a single, choreographed movement, the line of hoods silently moved into the house, and reemerged dragging the men from their beds. The men were thrown to the street, encircled by the crimson phantoms, the hollow faces looking down upon them, as the terrified men looked up in horror.

The leader stepped forward, once more, and stood over the two men, who were disrobed and shivering in the cold night air.

"*Serious charges have been brought against you,*" said that familiar voice.

One of the men tried to speak,

"*But we—*"

"*Silence!*" the leader overpowered him, "*you will not answer to me. Nor to anyone here.*"

He made a sweeping gesture to the crowd that had trapped them in.

"*You will answer to God.*"

He knelt down and leaned in, face-to-face with one of the men.

"*...And may He have mercy on your souls.*"

The hooded figure stood back up.

"*Let His will be done!*"

Shouting rang out, as the crowd moved in. I watched, just far enough away to stay hidden, but close enough to see what was happening. The men were castrated. It was horrific, I'd never seen so much blood. Their screams of pain, of terror, they were…sickening. The cheers became louder as one of the men drew his final breath, the other still holding on for dear life. As the leader knelt down, once more, to say something to the man…perhaps coaxing him to just give up, accept his fate, the dying man reached out and threw back the leader's hood. It was…"

She stopped.

"Who? Nora, who was it?"

"My grandfather. The very mayor of Hollingshead." Nora paused. "I was…*dumbfounded*. There *had* to be some mistake. I adored this man. He was kind. Soft and gentle. If I hadn't seen it with my own eyes, I never could've believed it to be true. I retched and threw up. I raced home, I had to beat them back. I had to tell my mother what I'd witnessed. She'd know what to do. She'd know how to make it right. Imagine my surprise, when I arrived home I found she and my grandmother waiting.

Without an ounce of hesitation, without stopping so much as to catch my breath, I tell them everything. I explain my theory that this must be what has happened to the Catholics, the former slaves, the immigrants, everyone who's been disappearing these last few years. But, instead of becoming as furious as I was, they just listened, quietly. When I'd finished, still breathing from the marathon I'd run, the endless stream of words I'd just thrown up at them, the women just looked at each other, then at me. *"Nora, darling, you mustn't tell anyone about this, do you understand me?"*

What? What did my mother mean? Surely they believed me. Didn't they? Turns out, they were already very aware that this was going on. In fact, it was something that had been going on for years. Long before I was born, before my grandfather had even been elected as mayor, it had started with my great grandfather.

"Why doesn't anyone put a stop to this? We have to stop this!"

I pleaded with them. They agreed, it wasn't right, but as women we must know our place, they said. We must know when to pick our battles. This wasn't a battle that we were fit to win. At least not in their measure. How could they just stand by? How were they content to remain silent? Knowing something wrong is going on and, and refusing to speak up, isn't that *just as wrong*? In my estimation it is.

But, I was alone in this. They made me vow to remain silent, which I did. I have all of these years, but made a vow to myself that I wouldn't rest until I had found a way to stop it. And more still, a way to somehow make amends. Though I knew that could never be done. Not to the extent it should be, but I had to try."

"What did you do?" Andie asked.

"I knew that, so long as my grandfather was mayor it would continue. And after his terms were up, my father would become mayor. Again, that solved nothing. But, maybe, just maybe *I* could be mayor. Then, I'd have the influence, the voice to really change things. Every election, I would try, and every election, I'd fail. No matter what I did, this town, this country just wasn't ready to see a woman elected into a position of leadership. So, *instead*, I took a position writing a column in the *Hollingshead Gazette*. Maybe I couldn't hold a political office, but I could inspire change through my words. The paper gave me a voice.

Little by little, I could feel the town shifting. Their narrow-mindedness, their hatred towards outsiders seemed to be waning. In the nineteen twenties, members of the *Klu Klux Klan* were so powerful that they were holding political positions within the state. But, only ten years later the organization was forced underground in the state of Maine. Their momentum was dying.

THE HAND THAT FEEDS YOU

The last known disappearance in our town happened in the late nineteen-eighties. Over the last few generations, this town has seen a surge of outsiders moving in, calling it their home. Diversity, while not as common as I'd like to see it, is becoming much more of a reality for us. That's why I encouraged Tilman to run for mayor in the last election. He has his faults, but he's a good man. He cares about this town. Everything he does, as mayor, is because it's what he believes is best to protect this town and its legacy."

"But you've chosen to keep silent about it? What about the victims? What about *their* voice?" Andie asked.

Nora walked across the room and opened a kitchen drawer. She returned with a notebook.

"What's this?" Andie asked.

Nora opened the front cover.

"It's a list of names. I've written the name of each and every one of them. I still speak their names. I talk to them. I'm not sure whether you believe in the spirit world or not, but I do. Tilman hates it, but it's something I really, truly believe in. I make sure they know that I remember them, that they're not forgotten."

She closed the notebook. Then went on.

"You probably think that's stupid," she said, looking

away; slightly embarrassed.

"Not at all. Nora."

Andie took her by the hand.

"Nora, I...I was wrong."

"About what?" Nora asked.

"About there being a story here."

"You mean, you aren't going to—"

"There are two stories here," Andie said, definitively.

"The first," she continued, "I am going to write about. About the girl, the house, the fire..."

"And the second?" Nora asked, afraid to know the answer.

"The second, *you're* going to write about."

"Me? Why *me*?"

"Because this isn't my story to tell, Nora. It's *yours*."

"Mine?"

"Think about it. The conviction you've felt to speak up...even after all of these years."

Andie grabbed the notebook from Nora's hands.

"You've kept a list of each and every one of their names. You talk to them. Nora, it's time to do more than that. It's time to set them free. It's time to set yourself free. Say their names. Give them their voice. Shed light on this town's past so that it, too, can start to heal. All of the time everyone's spent not talking about it, trying to pretend it didn't happen… that's not healing. That's only helping to protect the names… the legacies of those who are guilty, while the victims get nothing in return."

Nora was weeping now. Max and Sylvia could hear it on the recording.

"Nora…"

Andie lifted her chin so that their eyes met once more.

"Go with your gut."

CHAPTER 24

Julia was outside wrapping up her mums when Bennett came home.

"Is it gonna frost tonight?" he asked, carrying half a dozen grocery bags from the trunk.

"They're calling for it."

Julia stood up from her mums to give her husband a quick kiss. He dropped the bags on the ground and pulled his wife in tight.

"*Well*. Good afternoon to you *too*, Mrs. Taylor."

"Stop it," giggled Julia.

She was playfully trying to shove him away, but not enough that he'd actually let her go.

THE HAND THAT FEEDS YOU

"The groceries, babe, what about the groceries?" her words interrupted again and again as their lips locked.

"*Mmmm*. Sex and groceries. Who says being an adult's no fun?" Bennett laughed between kisses.

"The neighbors, they're gonna see us," Julia continued.

"Let 'em watch," Bennett smiled, "I like it. And I know *you* do *too*!"

"And Jordan? You know Jordan's home, right?" it was Julia's last rebuttal.

Bennett pulled away and looked at her.

"You want me to have him close up the shop tonight?" he said with a laugh, "we're his parents you know, we can do that."

"Get in there," Julia playfully shoved him off of her.

Satisfied that he'd gotten enough, at least enough foreplay, Bennett scooped up the grocery bags from the lawn.

"I expect to see those groceries put away by the time I get in there, *mister*."

She continued her playful scolding as he ventured inside.

"And I don't wanna see that you cracked a single one of those eggs!"

"Yes ma'am!"

Bennett's laughter rang from inside the house.

Sheesh. Julia laughed to herself, knowing full well that they'd finish their fun later tonight. Then she knelt down and went back to coddling her fragile flowers.

A black *Land Rover* pulled in the driveway, stealing her attention from the flowers once more. The SUV parked, the driver's door opened, and a chic pair of patent leather stilettos stepped out and determinedly strode up the driveway.

"Bennett!" Julia shouted.

"Uh huh?" even from inside the house, his boisterous voice carried.

"Come out here, please," Julia continued.

Bennett emerged from the front door, wiping off his hands.

"*Mrs. Bond,*" Bennett said, before reaching the last step.

"Hello Bennett. Julia. I was hoping that I might catch both of you at home. Might I have a word with you, both, please? It's very important."

"Of course," said Julia, "would you like to come inside? I've just made a batch of fresh apple cider. Should be cool enough to drink now."

"That sounds lovely, thank you," Nora said.

The trio made their way into the kitchen. Bennett and Nora sat at the breakfast table, while Julia prepared them all a glass of hot cider. The house was perfectly fragrant with the scent of warm apples and toasted cinnamon. Tasteful autumn decorations placed here and there, as only Julia could do. Her home was certainly her castle. Something that she prided herself in.

"Thank you," Nora said, as Julia sat a cup in front of her. Then continued, "I'm sure you're both wondering why I'm here."

Julia and Bennett looked at each other, then at Nora.

"Not really," Julia said.

"Oh?" said Nora, surprised.

"Well, I mean, we're only a few days away from elections. Paying house calls? If I had to guess, I'd say you're out securing votes," Bennett said, playfully.

"Well, you've got me *there*," Nora shrugged.

Everyone laughed.

"Julia, Bennett," Nora continued, "you know that *every* election is important. But I can't stress enough, just how important this upcoming election is—"

"Um, Mrs. Bond," Julia politely interjected, "I'll save

you the trouble. We couldn't agree more."

She looked at her husband, and went on.

"We think that Tilman has been a wonderful mayor, and you can rest assured that he'll have both of our votes this coming Tuesday."

Nora's face didn't look the way Julia had expected it to.

"Oh, well, I must say, I'm...very sorry to hear that," Nora replied.

The couple looked bewildered.

"I don't understand," said Julia.

"Tilman isn't running for re-election?" asked Bennett.

"No, he is," Nora replied.

"But, you *don't* want us to vote for him?" Julia asked.

"Personally, no. I mean, I'm *not* voting for him."

"Why not?" Bennett asked.

"Look, I'm going to be honest with you both. I love Tilman. He's a good man, and you're right, he's been a good mayor. He believes in this town and I know he'll continue to do what he thinks is best if he's mayor for another term. But," she looked earnestly at them, "but this town doesn't need more of the same ol' same ol'. You know?"

"Nora," Julia said, "you're not making any sense

here."

"Julia, you're a lot like Tilman. You know that?" Nora said, with a smile.

"I am? *How*?"

"You care so much about this town, it's your passion, your conviction to see it carry on, generation after generation. Never shaken, never scathed."

Julia looked perplexed. Was this an insult? She wasn't sure.

"But, this town needs to change," Nora went on. "*It has to change.* Julia, you know as well as I do that this town has worked hard to keep its past from getting out. Something that Tilman, and even you, have fought for; for years and years. And, for a time, I did too. I thought it was what we should do. Until one day, a writer came to town, and I know you both know who I'm talking about. She challenged me to do something bold. Something uncomfortable. Something I'd known that needed to be done, I just never could bring myself to do it."

"What's that?" asked Julia.

"I'm going to bring it into the light. Expose it. All of it. Every single detail."

She pulled the notebook from her purse and held it up.

"This is a list of every name, every victim that's disappeared over the years, as a result of this town's actions."

"Are you sure," Julia stopped then continued, "are you sure you wanna do this Nora? You're going to make some folks very angry."

"I've never been so sure. *Now* is the time. I'm going to publish the story in tomorrow's paper. I just wanted to give you both a head's up."

"What about Tilman?" Bennett asked.

"I'm sure he won't like it, but he'll get over it. Once the story breaks, he'll have no choice but to talk about it," Nora said.

"But, if not Tilman, who are you voting for as mayor?"

"That's right, he's running unopposed isn't he?" Julia asked.

"Well now, that's the thing, I do have a candidate in mind," Nora said. "Someone who could be written-in on the ballot."

"Who?" Bennett asked.

"You, Bennett."

"Me?"

Julia was equally surprised.

"Well, why not?" Nora asked.

"I can't think of any reason I should," he said.

"I can't think of any reason you shouldn't," Nora continued. "You're a successful entrepreneur, a family man, you've got charisma, people like you…"

"I don't know anything about politics," he said.

"Well, maybe that's just what this town needs, don't you think? Someone who's *not* a politician? Bennett, I think you're just the fresh breath of air this town needs. You'll bring young ideas. Change. Without a vision for the future, we're going to get stale."

"I still don't know," he said, thinking about it all.

"There is one more thing," Nora continued, "one more reason that I'd love to see your name on the ticket."

Nora set her notebook on the table, and opened it to an earmarked page. The page was filled with names, each written next to a number, keeping them all in order. She tapped the page on one particular name.

Bennett's eyes grew wide, and filled with tears. Julia saw his reaction, then leaned over to read the page for herself.

"What is it? Do you see someone you know?" she asked.

"My grandfather," he said, choking back on his

words.

Nora placed a hand on his.

"Bennett, this town didn't want your family to move in. To settle here. They'd hoped that by taking out your grandfather that your grandmother would be too distraught, unable to move on by herself, and that she'd just leave. But she proved them all wrong. Instead of caving in, she worked three jobs to single-handedly raise four children. Each of them she put through college. Encouraging them to make something of themselves. And each and every one of them did. They proved to her, and this town, that they were strong. That they were capable. And if that's not resilience, well then I don't know what is."

"Are you OK, honey?" Julia kissed her husband's forehead.

"Bennett," Nora brought him back to her conversation; she wasn't finished, not yet. "I cannot give you back what this town stole from you. But, what better way to show this town just how wrong they were about your family? The very family they tried to force out, now having its own flesh and blood holding the highest position in the town. Wouldn't that be something? I think it would."

She smiled at him.

"You really think I can win?" he asked.

"You've already got my vote," Nora replied.

"Well, this isn't just my decision."

He turned to Julia, and asked,

"I mean, what do you think? I won't do it if it's not something you're comfortable with."

Before she could answer,

"Do it."

All were taken aback by the voice that came from across the room. Jordan had been listening in on the entire conversation.

"Please, dad. It'll be the first election that I'm old enough to vote. I can't think of anything cooler than voting for my own dad."

Bennett's eyes welled up again.

"And besides, I think you'll make a great mayor," Jordan smiled, proudly.

After a moment, all eyes were on Julia.

"Well?" Bennett asked, "what do you think?"

"I mean…how can you argue with that?" Julia laughed, to keep herself from crying.

Bennett kissed her.

"And, he's right ya know," Julia went on, "you'll

make one *hell* of a mayor."

CHAPTER 25

Max was in the forest. The one that lay between the coastal road and Andie's car. He was sure of that much. He was dreaming. Or, at least the last thing he could remember was laying down at the hotel. But the air was cold. He could hear and feel everything, but he had to be dreaming, right? He hadn't driven up here. If he had, where was the car? Maybe if he pinched himself really hard, *holy fuckin' shit*! That was stupid. *OK*, so he could feel pain. And whoever started the rumor that you couldn't feel pain in dreams was a moron, because he'd just proved them wrong.

He looked around. He'd never been in this forest before, at least not outside of the car. Was Andie here? In the forest? Maybe they should've been looking here all along.

Maybe that's what she was trying to tell him. Why else would she bring him here?

"Andie!"

Nothing.

"ANDIE!!!"

An owl, on its suicide mission locked in on Max's head as its target. He jumped back, spooked.

Goddamn you, stupid thing!

Maybe he should lay off the yelling for a bit. Who knows, there might be wolves in these woods.

It was colder in the woods. He felt so tiny next to the rugged towers of trees. They seemed to be looking down upon him. Laughing at him, because his view of the very world around him was so limited, and they could see everything. Most of the deciduous ones had dropped their leaves, creating a soft carpet beneath his feet. All that remained had closed up their leaves for the night, to sleep. This allowed more light to penetrate the canopy, than was permitted during the daytime. Moonbeams, like large fingers, combed through the treetops, digging at the forest floor.

OK, well, no sign of Andie here. So, why am I here?

No sooner had Max thought this, a soft, gentle fog began gliding across the tops of his shoes. Then his shins.

And then his waist.

The fog. Of course, the house only appears in the fog!

He had to get to the meadow, before it was too late. But, which way was he supposed to go? To his left, his right, front and back, even with the dazzling moonlight, all he could see was trees. More and more trees.

Come on, Andie. Meet me halfway here.

That's when he heard it. *Was that?* Yeah, it *was*. *Music*. It was fucking music! In the middle of the woods. For a few moments, he walked in circles trying to pinpoint the direction the music was coming from. *That's it*, he thought, *it's this way*. He knew he was on the right path as the music grew closer and closer. Louder. Stronger. It was the sound of strings. Violins. An eerie waltz of some kind…echoing through the trees, like music that's heard from another room. Then came the light. He could see light now. Yellow, brilliant. The lights of a house peaking through the trees. He was so close.

Hold on, Andie. I'm coming.

As he emerged from the forest, stepping into the meadow, he stopped dead in his tracks. *Oh my god.* There it was. There it, fucking was. The house. But, not the house as he'd pictured it, or rather as the photo in the email had pictured it. No, the house was immaculate. It was beautiful, it was perfect. It stood three stories in some places; four in others. A thousand windows all ablaze with light. The facade was polished limestone, which gleamed against the countless luminaries that lined every walkway leading to the front entrance. Inside the windows, the front doors which stood wide open, Max could see people. Lots of them. They were having a party of some kind. A masquerade ball. Women in dazzling, embroidered ball gowns. Men in opulent, military dress regalia. All wearing masks to hide their faces.

The music continued to swell as Max cautiously approached the front steps. Within, he could see a procession of guest, walking arm in arm, up a marble staircase. Two doormen, also in masks, flanked either side of the open entrance. When they saw Max, neither said a word, but each hinged at the waist, bowing low; bidding him to enter.

For Andie, he bravely told himself; then, hesitantly, Max crossed the threshold.

Just inside the front door, a great hall stretched all the way up, and halfway back into the house. This was the nucleus, the epicenter, life's blood of the mansion. There was marble on top of marble. Polished marble, sparkling in the brilliant glow of the millions of candles that seemed to float everywhere, from the candelabras on stands to the mammoth golden chandeliers hanging overhead. Thick, crimson carpets stretched to and fro, showing guests their preferred path.

To his left, a long line of guests stood, ladies and their gentleman, arm-in-arm. Each awaiting their turn to make their way up the impressive marble staircase that lay just before him. They all seemed too lost in their own world to even notice Max was there. He took comfort in this. *Just gotta remain as inconspicuous as possible.* To his right, a large pair of ornately carved oak doors hung in their proud frame, like a priceless painting, wanting to be admired. Feeling severely under-dressed and with no mask to hide behind, Max opted to see what lay beyond the doors to his right. He carefully, and quietly opened one of the doors just enough to slip inside, then closed it behind him.

The room was a gallery, it seemed at least a mile long. It was just as bright as the great hall, but completely empty, well there were no people anyway. The red carpet at his feet stretched all the way to the far end. The ceiling was so tall that even the slightest move turned the hall into an echo chamber. He'd have to try even harder to keep quiet. To his right, the wall was lined with floor to ceiling windows, each framed with a pair of heavy, crimson drapes, trimmed with gold cord. To his left, an oak wall with coffered paneling stretched on and on, with an occasional chair or accent table serving as a mile marker, for the weary traveler that made their way from one end of the room to the other. Also on this wall, right in the center of the room, a large mirror, again trimmed in gold, stretched from the floor almost to the ceiling. Max had never seen anything like it in his entire life. He decided to go get a closer look.

Gliding slowly, gingerly, across the plush carpet, he made his way to the mirror and looked at his reflection. Despite the mirror's impressive scale, despite the real gold frame that enshrined it, the reflection was the same. *It's just a mirror*, he thought. Nothing truly spectacular, it does the job, same as any cheap copycat from *IKEA* would.

A white-gloved hand reached around from behind, and covered his mouth.

What the—?

He had been staring at his reflection the entire time. He could see the room behind him, the wall of windows. There had been no one there. And, no one came in, he would've heard them. So, *who* was this? *What* was this?

The hand spun him around with a force that almost knocked him off his feet.

THE HAND THAT FEEDS YOU

It was a woman. A beautiful woman, at least Max assumed she was, she was holding a mask over her face. She was sewn-into a ball gown, similar to all of the other ladies; except hers was red. Vibrantly red. Seductively red. *Sinfully* red. Her hair was red, too. Drawn up into a formal up-do, on top of her head, strands of diamonds and crystals weaved into her locks, with thick ringlets and curls hanging down here and there. The bodice of her dress was cinched until it was skin-tight. Its deep neck was slit, revealing the woman's breasts…at least an impressive amount of them. Her petite, swan like neck was celebrated by the opulent, diamond necklace that reverently bowed itself around it.

The only things about the woman that weren't red were her long, white gloves, and her porcelain mask, which stopped just shy of her seductive, pouting lips. These were, *of course*, red.

"What the fuck are you doing here?"

If it's possible to both scream and whisper at the same time, she had done it. At least, that's what it seemed like to Max. But, then, *Wait a minute*?!

"Andie?"

His voice was muffled, still trapped behind her satin glove. She slowly lowered her mask. It was *her*. It was Andie.

"Max, I'm going to let go now. But you have to promise me that you won't scream. You have to promise me that you'll be quiet. Got it?" Andie asked.

Max shook his head, still in disbelief. She dropped her hand.

"How did you find this place?" she asked, not really interested in the answer. "We have to get you out of here. You have to go, *now*."

"OK, then," Max whispered, "let's go. Come on."

He grabbed her hand and started to run, but she didn't move. She stood with such conviction that even Max, strong as he was, was pulled right back to her.

"What are you doing? Come, let's go," he said.

"No Max. You have to go," she said, "I'm staying here."

Max couldn't believe his ears. What was she saying? Didn't she know he'd been looking for her? Didn't she care? Wasn't she the one who'd brought him to this very spot? If not her, then who?

"I don't understand," he said.

"Max, you don't belong here. It's not safe–"

"And you do? *You* belong here?"

She looked down for a second, collecting her

thoughts, then back up at him.

"Yes, I do."

"This is bullshit—"

His words were cut off by the sound of the great, carved doors opening. Andie threw Max behind her to hide. Max couldn't see who entered the room, but whomever it was, must've been looking for Andie; because Andie spoke to them.

"Yes, I'll be right there," Andie called out.

There was a pause, then the doors closed.

"That was close. Do you realize how much trouble you could've caused, Max?"

She turned back to him, and continued.

"There's no way to get you out of here *now*. Not without you being seen."

Andie thought for a moment, then an idea struck her. She spun him back around so that he was once again face to face with his reflection in the mirror. Then, as he watched, she placed both hands over his eyes, paused for a second, then, like the grand drape being drawn back for the opening of a show in the opera house, her hands parted and Max's mouth dropped. Now, he too was dressed like the other gentleman waiting in the great hall. A svelte waistcoat, knee pants, stockings, a sword, the works.

"Not bad," Max laughed quietly, "we clean up pretty well."

"Here, take this," Andie handed him a mask. "Whatever you do, do *not* say a word to *anyone*, and do not, for any reason, lower your mask!"

Andie silently led him to the large, carved doors, the doors opened, seemingly by themselves, and the two of them stepped out into the great hall. The music had changed now, to a rigid, symphony of strings, full of mystery and intrigue, a Russian waltz, perhaps. The guests seemed to choreograph their every movement in tune with the music, carefully following its lead.

Max watched the guests, coupled together, making their way up the stairs, each relishing in the moment, making their grand entrance. The rise and fall of their step in perfect sync with each other. In perfect sync with the orchestra.

The next couple in line to ascend the stairs bowed low to Max and Andie. Bidding them to take their turn. Max knew it was Andie's intention to escort Max out the front door and safely out of this world. But, he wasn't here for that. He'd come for Andie and he wasn't about to leave without her. *Not a chance.*

THE HAND THAT FEEDS YOU

Max took Andie's arm and pulled her toward the stairs. He could feel her arm pull back in subtle resistance. He could feel her angry eyes upon him, even behind the mask, but he also didn't care. He knew the last thing she'd want to do is make a scene. To draw any sort of attention to them, so he didn't relent. Max led and Andie followed. Falling into procession, behind all of the other couples, and up the stairs.

The top of the stairs opened up into a magnificent ballroom, dripping with *Baroque* opulence. Gold, marble, carvings, statues, inlay, every detail of the room was more impressive than the last. The music was a full swell now as the couple reached the pinnacle of the stairs and made their way onto the dance floor, taking their position amongst the other guests.

The driving strings were stretching into an ominous and cunning waltz. The couples moved back and forth, around and around, the gentleman dipping their ladies, each moved slowly, seductively, like honey running down.

Andie locked eyes with Max as they danced. She was scolding him. For awhile she said nothing, then,

"You didn't answer my question," she finally said. "How did you find me?"

He quietly imitated a game show buzzer.

"Wrong. I'm sorry, the correct answer is, thank you Max, I'm so glad to see you. Let's get the fuck outta here."

"I already told you, I'm not leaving."

"Well then I'm not leaving either."

"That's stupid, Max. Don't be stupid. You have no idea what you're saying."

"I said I would take care of you Andie. This is me taking care of you. I came here to rescue you. And I can't even get a simple thank you."

"What makes you think I need you to rescue me?"

"Don't you?"

"Max, you've got to get out of here, before it's too late. Think of this as me rescuing you."

"I already told you, I'm not leaving here without you."

Max could see Andie roll her eyes. She was sticking to her guns. Why did she want to stay here? And why did he have to go?

"It's not worth it, Andie."

"What?"

"The story. It's not worth staying here, just to get this story."

"Max, you have no idea what you're talking about."

"Oh no? I know you Andie. You get obsessed when you're writing."

"That's not what this is, Max."

"I guess it's finally happened."

"What's happened?"

"You've fallen in too deep."

"Max—"

"You've went off the deep end, Andie. All of this, over a story."

"Don't you get it, Max? I haven't gotten lost in a story! I *am* the story."

"What?"

Silence.

"Andie, talk to me. What do you mean?"

More silence.

"Andie!"

What did he have to do to get through to her?

That's it, he quietly smiled to himself.

"Andie!"

Max stepped back and lowered his mask.

"Ah, good. I guess that got your attention."

The music had stopped now. All fell silent. All eyes were on them. Everywhere you looked a sea of white, porcelain faces.

"Max, please, no. You don't know what you're—"

Andie's desperate whispers were interrupted by one, solitary pair of hands applauding from across the ballroom.

Everyone turned to see who those hands belonged to. Then came the voice, ringing with laughter.

"Well, well, well. I heard we had an uninvited guest in our midst," the voice moved closer, carrying him with it.

The man was dressed like all of the other men, like Max, except he was in all black. From head to toe. Black. Except the mask he held over his face was gold, pure gold. It stopped just short of his lips. He smiled, a sinister smile.

"It isn't often we get someone brave enough, or, stupid enough to crash one of our little parties," he laughed.

His laughter boomed through the room, bouncing off every surface within it. Then came the laughter of the guests. All of them, *laughing*. But, it wasn't joyous laughter, it was, it was strange. It was bizarre. It was, terrifying.

The host smiled again. Max, knew that smile. He knew that...*voice*.

"Ray?" he asked the dark figure.

The gold mask dropped slowly.

It was him.

It was, *Ray*.

"Ray? What the fuck are you doing here?" Max asked, super-confused now.

"Max, you have to go, now!" Andie cried out from behind.

"Oh, you mean you haven't got it all figured out, already? Huh? Smart guy?" Ray sneered.

Figured what out? What the fuck's he talking about?

"Well, well, lookie here! The poor boy's confused. Aww…" Ray sighed, then his sigh turned to that devious laughter once again.

The guest's laughter erupted once more with his. But this time it was even worse. It was, it was *evil*. It was menacing. The sound of crazy people laughing. Like a crowded, psych ward, in an insane asylum. Their laughter turned to screeching. In an instant they all removed their masks, and, *holy shit*! Their faces were gone! All gone! Every last one of them a skeleton with rotting, dead flesh still clinging to its host. Their teeth were all canines. Gleaming. Sharp. They chomped and gnashed their teeth. Licking their lips, or what used to be lips. Ray did the same. His eyes growing wide.

"Max go!" Andie cried again.

The room began to change, the beautiful walls began to ignite and melt, until all was transforming, withering into mounds of ash. The guests, still laughing, were closing in on Max and Andie.

Andie grabbed Max this time and spun him around to face her. She was shaking him, desperately.

"Max, listen to me! You have got to wake up! *Wake up!*"

CHAPTER 26

"Max, Max wake up!" Sylvia said, shaking him.

"What, what the?" he sat up, slowly realizing that he was no longer dreaming. "What is it?" he finally asked, trying to catch his breath.

"You've gotta see this. Here, read it for yourself," she said.

He sat up and tried rubbing the sleep from his eyes.

Ugh. Reading? Right now, seriously?

She sat the morning copy of the *Hollingshead Gazette* in his lap.

There it was. An entire, front page feature. The title read: *Hollingshead, Digging Up the Past in Hopes to Find a Brighter Future. By Eleanor Bond.*

"Oh my god," Max said.

"She goes on to explain everything, in detail. The whitewashing. Those involved. And then, there's this."

She turned the page, revealing a list of names, then went on.

"She mentions all of them, every single one. Any poor soul who lost their life at the hands of this town, they're named right here."

"Wow. This is…just…wow," Max was speechless.

Sylvia turned it back to the article on the front page.

"She mentions Andie too," Sylvia continued, "thanking her for coming to this town. For opening up her eyes. For saving this town. And she really did, you know? None of this would've happened were it not for *her*."

"Yeah," Max almost choked on his words.

He guessed it was time to tell Sylvia about last night's dream, though he really had no idea what it meant. Andie had finally spoken to him, sure. But she didn't want to come back. And, come back from where? Where was she?

"Sylvia, I need to—"

"There's more," she stopped him.

"What?" he relented.

"I just went down to check out *The Festival of Leaves*.

Yeah, I know, lame, but whatever. Anyway, Bennett Taylor is running for mayor!"

"Mayor? Really?" Max asked. "Against Tilman Bond?"

"Mmhmm. And that's another thing, Nora is endorsing him!"

"Bennett?"

"Wrote a whole puff piece about him in the paper and everything. About why he'd be such a great mayor. The works."

"Wow."

"Yeah, you should see the crowd down there at his campaign tent. I think he might just win this thing."

Max shook his head. This was a lot of change happening, really fast. But it was worth it. It was time. This town needed it.

"*And it's all thanks to Andie,*" Sylvia said.

"Yeah, it's *all* thanks to *Andie*," he agreed.

CHAPTER 27

"Come on, Max! Hurry it up! Can't this thing go any faster?!"

Just like the last time the two of them had braved the long coastal road together, Max was the one driving the speeding getaway car. But, this time, Sylvia was the one calling all of the shots.

"The fog's rolling in! I don't wanna miss it. *Hurry*!" she demanded.

Max pushed the pedal to the floor and the turbocharger kicked in. Both of them were momentarily lifted from their seats by the speed, then softly touched back down.

They were driving so, disgustingly fast, that they both missed the slew of campaign signs in nearly every yard. Signs which read: *A Vote for Bennett Taylor is a Vote for Prosperity. A Vote for Progress.*

"OK, so, we get to the house then what?" Max asked.

"We bring her back!" Sylvia snapped, as if he were an idiot, as if he should've known.

"You really think she'll be there? I mean, that was all just a dream–"

"She's there. She's been there the whole time. We were just too stupid to realize it. Come on, go! Go!"

Sylvia was certain.

Max, not so much.

Yeah, he was willing to accept that there were some strange, supernatural forces at work here. Maybe even that this house was only visible in the fog. But, the thought of Andie being in this house the entire time? When he'd been to the very spot *twice*? No. No he would've felt her if she were there. He was sure of that much. Even in his dream, standing next to Andie, he could feel her. She was the one for him. His person. His other half. He didn't know if he truly believed in soulmates or not, but if they existed, Andie was his. No question.

The car sped along, teetering on the edge. Max watched for deer, and for the *holy shit!*

"Max, watch out!"

Sylvia threw her hands up over her eyes, as they, just barely, won their game of chicken with that stupid rock.

Every time. I swear that fuckin' thing moves, Max thought.

"That way! Hurry!" Sylvia shouted, as if Max didn't know. He was fully aware of their path by now. He'd been here, more times than Sylvia. This was why he didn't want her to come along, not up here, not tonight. He needed time to think about what he should do. What Andie meant by her words, if that was indeed *Andie* he'd talked to in his dream, and not just his subconscious having a bit of fun with his emotions.

The car climbed the rugged terrain once more, the valiant steed, charging into battle. The fog was still here, so maybe, *just maybe...*

"I see it! There it is, that's it!" Sylvia's face was pressed against the windshield, like a curious puppy.

She was right, though. There it was. Except, it wasn't. Not as Max had seen it in his dream. There were no lights. There was no music. No guests milling about. It was just the ghost of the house. It's charred walls, crumbling ruins of their former glory. Its vacant windows staring down at them as the

Volvo inched closer and closer to it. Moonlight shined upon the roof, penetrating the gaps left behind by the fire, and danced about its hollowed interior. The house had a presence, that was for damn sure. It was watching them. It had been waiting for them. For the first time since leaving the hotel, Max felt afraid.

Max parked the *Volvo* next to Andie's car and turned off the ignition.

"Sylvia, maybe you should wait here."

"Wait here? Are you kidding? Hell no. I'm going in with you."

She wasn't about to take no for an answer.

"The floors are likely rotted. It could be dangerous."

"Max, listen to me."

Sylvia looked at him tenderly, so much so that Max wondered if he might still be dreaming. Who was this woman? She went on,

"I don't know what we'll find in there. We might find Andie, and I *pray* that we *do*. But, we don't know if she'll be–" she stopped herself, then tried once more, "there's a chance that she'll be…" she trailed off again.

"*Dead*," Max said. "I know, that's something I've had to come to terms with."

"I just don't want to see you have to face that *alone*. Not after what you went through, losing your dad. Max, I wanna be there for you, just in case, *OK*? Whatever happens, we'll see it through, *together*."

Max was touched. Almost moved to tears. Sure, it was no secret that he'd taken to the old bat, but more than that, he loved her.

"OK," he said, "let's go."

The two of them opened their car doors, turned on their phone's flashlights, then stepped out into the cold, dark night. Standing next to it, the house had a vibration that could be felt. Not just by Sylvia, but by Max as well. It had a presence all its own, an energy. Max took her by the hand.

"Come on," he whispered as they made their way up the front steps, tiptoeing so as not to disturb the house, to awaken it from its dark slumber.

The splintering door seemed sturdy, but it had been weathered by the years, and proved to provide little resistance when Max pushed against it. And just like that, they drew in a deep breath, and ventured inside; each certain that they might never come back out.

The layout of the house was just like in Max's dream. They felt desperately inferior, against the scale of the great hall. Candelabras still stood around the room, like wallflowers at a ball, but completely devoid of candles, devoid of light. Everything was covered in dark layers of soot and ash. Covered in death.

Max noticed something shining on one of the treads of the marble staircase. He ventured over to get a closer look.

"She's been here," he whispered.

Even in hushed tones, his voice echoed throughout the chamber. Sure enough, there was Andie's signature, drawn into the ash that covered the step, exposing the exquisite, polished marble that had lain dormant underneath. Max smiled as he looked at it, taking the image of it into his mind. This wasn't a dream, this was real. Andie had been here. Andie *was* here. He could feel her presence again.

"See, Sylvia?" he turned around to point out his findings to her, only, she was gone.

"Sylvia? Sylvia?" he whispered into the darkness.

Silence.

Max drew in a long sigh.

Great, now I've gotta find two women in this house.

He thought of the first place he'd seen Andie in the house. Maybe she was waiting for him in the gallery. That's where he'd start. Instinctively, he turned to his right and shined his flashlight in his path. Slowly, he crept closer to the heavy oak carved doors. When he'd reached them, he tried turning the handle, but the doors were stuck. Or, maybe locked? Still, the front door was no challenge, so why should these give him any trouble? Again he turned the handle and threw all of his weight into the door.

Crash! The doors fell out of their casing and came barrelling down to the floor in a thundering blast. Max jumped back to keep from getting crushed. *Surely Sylvia heard that*, he thought. *Surely Andie heard that.*

As the dust settled, Max peered inside the gallery, permitting his flashlight to lead the way once more. There it was, the once opulent mirror, now looked grotesque. Just like the house, it was now broken, and horrible. "*Come to me, Max,*" he could almost hear it say, "*look into me.*" Again, looking into it the last time is what brought Andie to him, so *maybe*?

It was a noble thought, but it didn't work. Max stood there. For a solid minute he stood there. He stared at his reflection. The blinding flashlight of the phone, as it was reflected back at him from the mirror's surface. An unwanted gift that it blatantly rejected. Darkness reigned here, *now*; the light wasn't welcome.

"*Hahahaha,*" a child's laughter broke through the silence.

Startled, Max dropped his phone; luckily it didn't break. He bent down to pick it up, and shine it in the direction of the girl's laughter, just to catch a glimpse of her running away, leaving the cavity from the oak doors empty once more. He could hear her laughter continue into the great hall, then travel, along with a small pair of footsteps, up the marble staircase.

"Wait a minute! Come back here, please?!" Max urged in a fervent whisper.

He found himself in the great hall once more, standing face to face with the grand staircase.

What the fuck am I doing? Chasing a little demon child up the dark scary stairs? Sure, Max, why not? he laughed ironically to himself.

Inch by inch, he made his way up the stairs. With each step, he could hear the echo of the child's laughter.

It's coming from the ballroom. She's in the ballroom!

As he reached the top of the stairs, Max shined his flashlight about the large room.

"Hello? Little girl, are you in here? My name is Max. Are you, Bella? Is your name *Bella*?"

No response.

"I'm not gonna hurt you, *OK*? I just wanna talk to you? I'm looking for a friend of mine. I think she might be in here. Have you seen her?"

Each step took him closer to the center of the room; a room where guests had once dressed in their finest, and festively-waltzed the night away. *But no longer.* The music, the guests, all were gone; faded into silence. Now, the only ones dancing in the room were the floating dust particles, which suspended themselves, in the time and space of this, long-forsaken venue. Things that, like everything else in this cursed house, shielded themselves within the safety of the desolate, dark shadows. Exposed only amidst the delicate pools of light, created by the intruding moonbeams; which now blatantly haunted the space. Moonbeams which tore through the large, arch-top windows, that framed the far side of the ballroom. Windows that looked out; holding hopeful vigil, upon the world below. The world of the *living*.

There! In the middle of the room! A dark shape, maybe a figure? It was sitting in the middle of the dance floor.

"Hello?"

Again, no reply.

"Bella? Is that you?"

Max crept closer still.

"Andie?" he said, hesitantly.

He was close enough now that he could see it, or he'd be able to, if he shined his light on it. For a moment, he wasn't sure he wanted to. He didn't know if he wanted to see it or not. It wasn't moving, whatever it was. Slowly, very slowly, he lifted his light to force the thing to reveal itself.

"Ahhh!" he screamed, not even caring how much noise he made.

His scream echoed through the ballroom, down the marble steps, and even out the front door of the house.

"Sylvia! Oh, god, *no*. Sylvia!"

He quietly wept at the sight of his dead friend. Her throat slit from ear to ear, not a clean slice either, more like something had savagely eaten the flesh away. Her eyes still open, fixed in horror, terrified by whatever they'd last seen, mouth wide open, poised and ready to scream. To scream for Max to come and help her, no doubt.

"Oh, Sylvia, I'm so sorry."

For a moment, Max thought about running. There'd be no shame in that. Whatever this was, it wasn't human. It was OK to be scared. It was OK to run. Hell, it probably made the most sense anyway. I mean, who was *he* to go up against this, this, whatever the fuck it was? Max didn't even know what he was facing here. The thing *clearly* outranked him.

But, without Andie, his life had no meaning. He had his mom, sure, and of course he loved her. But, a world without Andie, that just didn't sound like a world he wanted to live in. If he couldn't rescue her, if he couldn't bring her back, then he'd die trying.

"Alright, motherfucker! Where are you, huh?"

He began shouting as he turned to leave the ballroom.

"Are you down here?"

He waved his flashlight down a long, dark corridor.

"You think I'm afraid of you, huh? I'm beginning to think it's you who's afraid. Why don't you come out and show yourself, huh?"

He was talking macho, sure, but it was all an act. Max was terrified. Like, shit your pants terrified. But, accepting that lackluster level of confidence wouldn't carry him very far. Not in this horrible place. So he faked it.

The girl's laughter came from close behind him. Max spun around, and heard the laughter retreat into a room with an open door. He followed after it.

The center of the room was bright. Thanks to the large windows and the daring moon; which forced its way into the room through every opening it could find. This, however, cast heavy shadows around the perimeter of the room. Encasing the entire edge of the room in a thick veil of darkness.

It was a child's room. Max could tell by the fragments of charred toys that lay about. A large bed, or what was left of it, still took up residence in the center of the room; bathed in moonlight, practically begging someone to come lay on it.

"This was my room," the girl whispered from behind.

Max almost screamed he was so startled; but in an instant, he collected himself and put on that brave facade once more.

"I know who you are. You're Isabella Cartwright, aren't you?"

The girl looked at him, but said nothing.

"They called you Bella, didn't they?"

A look of sadness washed over her face. For a moment, Max didn't know whether he was supposed to be feeling afraid, or pity for this child. It was a demon, right? Could they have feelings?

Come on, Max. Get a hold of yourself. "Stay

skeptical," remember?

Trust no one.

Trust nothing.

"I did something bad," she said; her voice bearing even more sadness than her face.

"I know what you did," Max said, gravely.

"You...do?"

More sadness on that little face, and, what was that? Were they tears?

She's playing you, you idiot! Snap out of it!

Max felt himself slipping further and further away from reality; lost in her trance. He'd have to keep laser focused if he had any chance of getting out of here *alive*. He thought of Sylvia. The ancient history of this house was one thing, but this hellish creature had just killed his friend. He was sure of it. He was also sure that, if he wasn't careful, he'd be next.

"You killed my friend!" he shouted, rage pouring out of him. *Yeah, that's how it's supposed to feel. Keep going, Max.*

"I didn't!"

"In the ballroom, I saw you!"

"But I didn't—"

"I know it was you!"

He lunged toward the thing, not really sure what he was going to do if he actually reached her. The creature turned away and ran into the dark shadows of the room, screaming,

"I didn't do it!"

"But *I* did!" came the voice from the darkness.

It wasn't the girl's voice. This was a man's voice. Booming with resonance, with absolute power, yet shrill at the same time...like the breaking of glass or nails on a chalkboard. As it spoke, its breath stained the darkness; faint wafts of hot vapor triumphantly battling against the cold night air. Max's blood went cold.

"Who's there? Who are you?" Max tried his best to sound brave.

A marginal effort. Inside, Max was trembling.

"Ah," said the voice, "you mean you don't know? I thought *you* knew everything."

"Whatever you are, I'm not afraid of you! Show yourself. Come and face me, like a man!" Max demanded.

He'd be sorry he commanded the thing to show itself. Such a creature is better left in the shadows. Out of sight. The first thing that came was the sound of something heavy, being dragged across the floorboards. Then, he could see it. It was a hoof. Like that of a large goat. Polished black, gleaming in the moonlight, with equally polished ebony fur climbing the leg of it. Inch by inch, it moved out of the shadows, until Max could see all of it.

It stood taller than a man. It wasn't a man, but, some part of it was. The lower extremities were that of a goat. Strong haunches propped it up. Above the waist, it was human, sort of. Its muscular chest was hairless, but just as jet black as the rest of the beast. Its arms were equally as strong as the rest of it, with bulging biceps leading to vascular forearms…until the wrists, where, instead of hands, it was fitted with a three-pronged claw, trimmed with razor sharp blades for fingernails. Two onyx horns extended up and outward from its broad head. For the face, it was a mixture of the two, man and beast. Blazing, golden eyes, inlay with black pupils, a furry black snout, and a human mouth; which possessed a full set of gleaming white canines. It was…in a word…terrible.

Whatever you do, Max, do NOT let this thing sense your fear.

Though, he figured, if the beast couldn't hear it in his voice, or his racing heartbeat, it could probably smell the piss that Max was unable to contain in the instant that he first saw it; in all of its horrible glory.

"How about now, are you afraid now…Max?"

Several things caught Max's attention at that very moment.

First, the thing knew his name. How in the hell was that possible?

Secondly, as the thing spoke, or rather, hissed, its forked tongue fluttered about and lapped at its deadly fangs; like a venomous snake. Those teeth, it loved to bear its teeth. It was smiling. A smile so familiar. Which brought Max to the third thing. He knew that smile. That, cacophonous laugh. He'd heard it, time and time again.

"Still not afraid?" the creature laughed again.

The reverberations cracked through the room, through the cavernous house, like a leather whip.

"Afraid? Of you? Not a chance," Max lied through his teeth.

"Just you wait."

Its laughter rang out once more.

OK, Max. It's now or never.

"If you say so. *So*, do you go by *Satan*?" Max paused, "or…should I just call you *Ray*?"

The creature stopped laughing.

Before Max's very eyes, the thing dropped its furry facade, like a heavy winter coat, taking a more-familiar, human-form. Max now found himself standing face to face with Ray.

"Well, well. Look who finally joined the party. Maybe he's not so stupid after all," Ray laughed.

Those perfect white teeth. That devilish charm on full display once more. Seeing him now, in this place, knowing who he really was, Max wasn't sure if he would rather stare at the terrible beast or the cocky, annoying creature that used to call him *friend*.

"What are you doing here? What are either of us doing here? And, where the fuck is Andie?" Max pressed him.

Ray laughed.

"My, my. You *are* demanding. It's adorable watching you squirm. Not having any of the answers. Look at poor Max! The wannabe know-it-all, now just a bumbling idiot. You know, this is why I came. This is why I'm here! I've been watching you for years. Ever since day one, I've thought of this day. Of this, very moment. I've never hated someone so much. And, that's saying something, Max. That's gonna make your death all the more enjoyable."

"So, what, you've brought me all the way here to kill me? Seems like an awful lot of trouble. Why not just do it? Get it over with?"

Max threw up his hands. For a moment, he forgot he was talking to the Devil *himself*. He and Ray had so much history, it made it easier to let his guard down. If Ray hated Max, Max certainly had lots of pent-up hatred for him too. The annoying nicknames. The incessant talking. The lame jokes. All of it.

"Why? To watch you suffer, of course! Yes, I could've just killed you that very first day. You know how painful it's been having to deal with your bullshit for all these years? The arrogance. The ego? That's when I decided to use you as part of my plan. All this time, you were just a pawn, and you had no idea. That's what made it all worthwhile. Watching you make an idiot out of yourself, all the while, you had no idea."

"So you decided to kill the woman I love? Just to watch me suffer?"

Max's accusations may've been hurled at Ray, but Max was the one who felt the full strength of their truth. Andie was dead, because of *him*. He thought of that night at the bar, where he said he'd protect her, no matter what; give her whatever she needed, just like she'd done for him the night of his dad's funeral. Now, she was gone, and it was all because of him.

Ray threw his head back and laughed, that foul laugh that displayed all of his teeth. Max felt like Ray must've known how much he hated that goddamn laugh, that's why he chose to whip it out in this moment.

"You really don't have a clue, do you?"

"OK, fine, Ray! You win, I give up! Humor me! Tell me what the fuck is going on here!"

Max's blood was boiling now. If he was gonna go down, he was gonna do it in a blaze of glory.

"The woman you love? You have no idea what you're talking about. You don't know anything about her."

Ray reached into the shadows, and pulled the girl out by the hand; whipping her around to his side.

"Bella? What does she have to do with any of this?" Max sneered.

"Oh, I'm sorry, you don't know her as Bella..."

Ray's words trailed off, as he threw a glance down at the girl. In an instant, she began to levitate, then as she hovered in the emptiness of the room, her limbs stretched, then her torso, her curly golden locks grew and swelled into that familiar shade of auburn, and lastly, her face transformed into...

"Andie?!"

Max couldn't believe it.

She gently floated down, taking her place next to Ray.

"Ding, ding, ding! He finally got one, ladies and gentleman! Tell the audience what he's won," Ray mocked.

Andie looked pitifully at Max. But she didn't say a word. For the first time, Max wondered if Andie's feelings toward him had all been an act, too. Had Ray been using her to get close to him? It made sense. But, his gut told him that it couldn't all have been an act. No, there was something there. And, if he was gonna die today, he'd at least get her to admit it.

He deserved that much, didn't he?

"Why Andie? Why did you lie to me? And how—" Max's words were cut off by Ray.

"Oh, I know this one! Here, you sit tight, babe. Lemme explain it all to him."

Ray stretched out an arm, and commanded a chair to come sweeping in from the shadows. Another wave of his hands, and Andie was forced into the chair, unable to move.

Unable to speak.

"See, you know about the history of this house. Her mother, her true mother, felt somewhat responsible for the tragedy caused by her daughter. After all, the girl had been manipulated by all of the adults around her. All in hopes that she would love them," Ray shuddered at the notion. "Ugh, love. What a perfectly terrible concept. Makes us do the stupidest things. So, since she knew the child's soul would be damned, cursed to burn for eternity because of her sins, the mother made a deal with…well, with *me*. Ha! In exchange for her soul, the girl's purpose in life would now be to bring me countless souls in exchange for hers. See, I've always been one with an eye for a bargain, and, what's one soul, if you can have many in its place? So, I agreed."

"But, Bella, Andie, they're not the same person—"

"Oh, that. You noticed, eh?" Ray turned to Andie, "maybe he's not so dumb after all, *huh babycakes*?" he laughed, then turned back to Max. "No, you're right. She's human. Mortal. Which means she can die. But, if she dies, she can't stay dead, right? I mean, her soul's gotta go somewhere," he laughed again. "And, well, a deal's a deal. Even for me. So, she has to come back each time. The problem is, each time, she's born a new life. Her sins are still there, but she doesn't remember it. Any of it. She has to be reminded. I've got to tell her—"

"Through her dreams!" Max stopped him.

Ray threw up a hand, and a piece of duct tape appeared over Max's mouth.

"I'm the one telling this story. Please don't interrupt. *It's rude*. Now, as I was saying…*yes*…through her dreams. I always reveal myself to her when she's a child. But, this time, her parents sent her off to that miserable place, and she learned how to control her dreams. She was so good at it, that even I couldn't get through to her after a time. So, she grew up not knowing."

Ray stopped, looked back to Max, and smiled a devious smile.

"Then, one day, I met *you*. And suddenly I knew what I'd do. It would all be perfect. A way to reach Andie and a way to make you suffer in the process. Now she knows. And I've got you here. Normally I don't show up to these things, but in your case I thought I'd make an exception."

Max almost fainted as his mind finally connected all of the dots. Ray was right, he was a pawn. He felt like a fool. I mean, he couldn't have known. But, still. He looked at Andie.

I guess it all was just an act. An act to make me feel stupid. To make this moment even more painful.

Max ripped the tape off of his mouth.

"Alright, Ray. I guess killing me is the last part of your plan, huh? You've watched me suffer. So, just get it over with. Go ahead and kill me, I won't put up a fight."

The devious laugh returned one last time.

"Kill *you*? I'm not going to kill you, Max."

"But, I thought—"

"I killed your father…"

Max took these words as a gut punch. His mother was right. His father hadn't died of natural causes; but rather, supernatural. Max promised himself, *if he got out of this alive*, he'd go with his mom to her next session. He owed her that much.

"But you?" Ray continued, "killing you would be *too* easy. Where's the fun in that? No, Max, I'm not gonna kill you."

Ray looked over at Andie, and lifted his hand. She stood up.

"She's gonna kill you," said Ray.

"*Andie*? She wouldn't—"

"Oh, but she *would*. She **will**. She has to do *anything* I command her to do. A deal's a deal," he hissed.

Andie walked obediently forward, and took Max by the arm, leading him out of the room, down the hall, and down the grand staircase. From the top of the stairs, Max could see the flickering of candles, and a large pentagram traced onto the marble floor in the center of the room below. This was where it was all going to go down. She was going to steal Max's soul.

He really did feel stupid. Ray had won in every way. What hurt the most was that he had fallen for Andie, but the whole time, she was only playing him. Using him. *Right*? She had to've been using him. Everything else Ray said made sense. But, Max still couldn't shake the feeling in the pit of his stomach. Maybe it was just hopeless optimism. Or, maybe, *just maybe*, he was *right* about one thing. *Maybe, Andie really did love him.*

"Don't do this, *please*," he quietly whispered as she slowly led him down the stairs; certain that Ray was trailing behind them.

"I tried to warn you Max. Time and again, but you wouldn't listen."

That's right. She did try to warn me. See? She does have feelings for me.

"Andie, listen to me, you don't have to do this, OK?"

"Of course I do, Max. I have to do *anything* he says. I don't have a choice."

"But this isn't you."

"You've seen all that's happened, Max. You've heard everything. I've killed people. Lots of people."

"But that wasn't you," he quietly pleaded, "well, it was but…it wasn't. Not *you*. Not the *Andie* that I know. The Andie that I know, is a fucking talented writer. Her stories are loved by *millions* of people. The Andie that I know came to this town, searching for a story and instead found that this town was broken; buried beneath a century of its own wrongdoings. And, because of her, because of her desire to do the right thing, she convinced the town's own, mayor's wife, to expose the truth; to give a name and a voice to each and every one of the victims that it took. And, because of *her*, the town is about to elect Bennett Taylor as its very first black mayor."

He looked her in the eye. Her eyes were filled with tears, tears she'd been trying to hold back, but couldn't.

"Bennett? He's going to become mayor?" she asked in a whisper.

"All thanks to you. That's the Andie I know."

THE HAND THAT FEEDS YOU

She contemplated this, silently.

Max thought she was going to tell him that he was right, that she wasn't going to kill him after all. That they'd somehow manage to fix this horrible mess, together, or at least they'd die trying. But she didn't.

"Max, you fell in love with a killer. I've killed before, I'll kill again. I've been working with Ray to bring you here, to steal your soul. That's why I've been coming to you in your dreams. I'm a monster, can't you see that? You have to see that. If you don't then, you're dumber than Ray gives you credit for."

Max thought for a moment, then,

"Maybe you're right. Maybe all of that is true. And I may be an idiot, because none of that changes a thing. I still love you, even if you kill me, take my soul, I'll still use my last breath to say that I love you, *Andie Sterling*. I've never loved anyone else, but I love you. And I'll give you my life, if that's what it takes."

When they reached the bottom of the stairs, she took Max by the arm and forcefully threw him to the ground.

"Over there, into the circle," she commanded him.

Ray had descended the stairs, and took his position, perched upon a gilded chair; that had somehow been spared by the fire over a century ago. His eyes dancing with delight, his smile permanently plastered across his face.

Max was laying on his back, in the center of the circle, now. Andie knelt over him, ripping his shirt open, displaying his bare chest. She drew a gleaming sword from the floor next to her. She looked down at him.

Even in this moment, even when his heart was racing at the thought of her slicing him open like a frog in some eighth grade biology class. Even with her face resolute, as if she felt that this was all perfectly routine; something she'd already done, hundreds of times, something she'd do again plenty of times more. He couldn't help but see every moment they'd shared together playing back in his mind. The moment when his life was supposed to flash before his eyes, it wasn't the extended director's cut, it was the abridged version, curated with only the best moments they'd had.

If looking up at her was going to be the last thing he saw in his life, then it had all been worth it.

"Goodbye, Andie. I will always love you."

He closed his eyes tight, bracing for impact, when,

"Ugh," she quietly murmured, "fine, Max, you win. I won't do this. I can't."

He opened his eyes.

I knew it! She does love me!

He smiled.

"We'll think of something. There *has* to be some way out of this—"

"Max don't you think I've tried? A dozen lifetimes and I'm still here. There is no way out. *Unless…*"

"Unless what?"

"I just accept my fate. Let my soul go where it's supposed to go."

"No, Andie, that's not going to happen."

"Max there is no other way."

An idea came to him.

"Wait a minute, he said himself, he loves a bargain. Let's make him an offer he can't refuse."

"But, Max, I don't have anything he wants."

Max swallowed hard, then,

"But *I* do."

"What's taking so long?!" Ray's voice boomed like an explosion, echoing from every solid-surface in the great hall.

"You know, Ray, I've been thinking," Max sat up, casually.

His words easy, his tone even, as if this were just some perfectly ordinary day's conversation. Before Ray could answer, Max continued.

"I know you're a guy who loves to make deals. So, I've got a proposal for you."

"*You?*" Ray scoffed, "you've got *nothing* I want!"

"What if, instead of having Andie kill me, you let me take her place instead?"

"Max, no—!" Andie shouted.

"Ha! Nice try, but I'd rather watch her take your life," Ray snapped.

"Think about it, Ray! Think about how much you *hate* me. I'm a smart-ass. A know-it-all., I know how much that gets under your skin."

Ray's eyes narrowed.

"But," Max continued, "if Andie kills me, then that's it. My suffering's over."

Max thought for a second about what he was just about to say, then,

"But if you let me take her place, then, you'll have me for an eternity. I'll become your slave. I'll be bound to do whatever you say. To play the fool to you each and every day, forever and ever. And there'll be nothing I can do to ever be free of it. I'll be miserable for all eternity."

Ray was definitely considering this.

"From where I'm sitting, that sounds like a better deal to me, or maybe that's just because I know better than you do—"

Max knew that was a risky statement, but he also knew that if anything sealed the deal, calling himself smarter than Ray was just the thing to convince the bastard that it was worth it.

"Enough!" came his thunderous reply. "Alright, Max, you've intrigued me…"

"Max, no. Please, you don't have to do this," Andie whispered in his ear.

"But, you have to promise me that Andie will be free. She'll be free to go on, living her life."

Max turned to her, she was silently weeping.

"And," Max continued, "whenever the day comes that she does die, her soul will be able to go wherever is fit for the actions of *her* life. No one else's. *Deal*?"

He extended a handshake to Ray.

After another moment of deliberation, Ray simply said,

"Deal."

Just then, a mighty wind came rushing through the hall.

One by one, the marble blocks that comprised the concentric, circular pattern of the floor dropped to the center of the earth; exposing a massive, round chasm. Max looked at the hole in horror, the thought of jumping into this bottomless pit was the least of his worries; but he didn't regret his decision. He'd do it all again, in a heartbeat. This…was for Andie.

"What are you doing Max?" she asked, grabbing his arm.

"ONE!" Ray shouted.

"I told you I'd give you whatever you needed. This is me making good on that promise."

"TWO!"

"Max, I can't let you do this!" she quietly pleaded.

"THR—"

Before Ray could say *three*, Max, who stood face to face with the portal, eyes-closed, ready to jump, felt a strong grasp on the back of his arm, then a yank that sent him flying backwards, sliding across the floor and away from the hole.

What the—?

Then he saw Andie, step forward, taking his place, taking…*her place*. Then, she jumped in, just as the hole sealed itself back up; leaving everything as it had been before.

Silence.

Dead. Silence.

"NO!" Max shouted.

But it was too late.

Ray was gone.

Andie was gone.

Max was now the only living soul, in the empty house.

For a moment, he just sat there. He finally understood what it felt like to be in the mind of Pete Mcmanus, the patient from the asylum. For in this moment, reliving all that he'd just witnessed, he *too* merely *existed*. Motionless. Silent. Trying to wrap his head around it all. Did all of this really just happen? Was he dreaming again?

Please say that it was all just a dream.

But it wasn't. Eventually the pain of reality set in, and Max wept. He wailed. His cries rang out into every square inch of the house, until they sliced through every crack in the outside walls, every open window, and spilled into the angry sea below.

The front doors opened, and Max stepped outside, into the warmth of the looming sunrise. Trying his best to focus on the positives. He was still alive. He'd faced the very Devil *himself*, and lived to tell the tale. The morning felt so new, so full of promise. But, the long trek to his *Volvo* was a lonely one.

In the days and weeks that followed, Max would gather his thoughts into a handful of journals. Eventually, he'd write them into a book, titled: *The Hand That Feeds You*. It was his story.

It was *my* story.

It was *our* story.

You know, a friend once told me that writing horrific experiences into a work of fiction was cathartic; because those stories no longer existed in our reality, but it's not true.

It'll *never* be true.

Not for *me*.

Because the woman I loved is gone.

Forever.

THE END.

ACKNOWLEDGMENTS

The author of this book would like to express their warmest gratitude for the following person(s); without whom, this book would not be what it is.

First, to all of the literary agents who didn't believe in this book, thank you. Your rejection encouraged change and tenacity. And to all of the literary agents who did believe in it, your encouragement inspired this story to keep going; certain it would find its way, somehow.

Secondly, to the baristas at my local Starbucks, thank you. Thank you for allowing me to spend hours, upon hours, in your store; editing, revising, and never calling me weird for the time I spent there. At least, not to my face.
In the same vein, to my local coffee shop, Espresso Laine, you are, and forever will be, my favorite local haunt. Thank you for being a sounding board, and my champion, throughout this journey.

Third, Old Britney. You know who you are. Your faith in me helps me to dream bigger. Your sarcasm keeps me grounded. Thank you. I'll see you soon.

Fourth, to all of my beta readers and editors. Thank you. I'm humbled that you took the time to help me tell this story.

Lastly, if you purchased this book, a million times over, I'd like to say, thank you. Writing this story has been a dream come true, and the fact that you've shown your support, by purchasing a copy, means the world to me. I hope that you've enjoyed it.

Made in the USA
Las Vegas, NV
01 April 2024